Based On True Events

Watson

A Novel

By

Abraham Gabriel Pagtama

ISBN: 978-0-578-47981-1

Published by

Abraham Gabriel Pagtama and Associates

ABRAHAM
GABRIEL
PAGTAMA
& ASSOCIATES
PUBLISHINGS

Dedicated to my father Abe, my mother Rhoda and sister Karen.

Thank you God my love and savior Lord Jesus Christ.

CONTENTS

1

The Historical Significance of these Events

In the days of the 1930's era it was well known that there were over thirty-five thousand Filipinos mostly skilled farm workers living in America with the highest concentration residing in the Central Valley area of California. This was where the majority of Filipinos in the United States lived during this time of American history.

At a present day news press conference with one of the only known living survivors of that time Filipino American Monong, Christian Portugal Abad, an original farm worker, in his three piece suit, slicked backed hair that is slightly balding because his hair is thinning out, chubby like a big teddy bear, wearing glasses because he is crossed eyed in his left eye from being born with the condition called strabismus; along with calluses still on his hands from his hard life experiences working on the farm fields holding on to the microphone like he is a karaoke singing champion, he is known as a former dancer, dance instructor, Hollywood actor when they need a character who looks like him, a bonsai master, producer, top chef, speaker, entrepreneur, retired U.S. army and airforce veteran of ninety years of age all grey haired sitting in a chair, he is being interviewed by television network, newspaper reporters and media production crews about his life on the farmlands when he first arrived in America.

"Ok any questions remaining for Mr. Abad?" Shouted the host for the evening Isaiah Boyet Carino a Filipino publicist for the Philippine Mega Globe newspaper wearing his brand like circle cola bottle looking glasses and sporting a tapered grown mustache and little stubble beard at the tip of his chin looking like a director he says, "Ok thanks, you ma'am go ahead what is your question?"

"Monong Christian please tell us how you feel about your life now as compared to your life when you first came to work in America during the era of the nineteen thirties." Asked Janet Neubauer an American Filipina German journalist reporter with brown hair looks mestiza she is from the local westside daily outlook newspaper wearing a nice pink dress and sun hat covering the light glowing through the window pane glass shining upon her brown eyes.

"I have to tell all of you... you all have it so good! Do you know what we discovered when we first came to America? We discovered that we were treated like animals! Treated like dirt! Like dirty dogs! Have you seen what a dirty dog looks like? Let me tell you this story boys and girls that I am sure you will love based on true events I have seen it with my own two eyes, smelled it clearly with my flat nose and heard it with my own two big elephant ears!" Declared Christian.

Back on the nineteen thirties era Batac Philippine Ilocos Norte farm fields at the rise of the early dawn morning island sun. Joe Billy American, a blue eyed brown hair tall bearded white American agricultural laborer recruiter with his sombrero hat is in the Philippines to recruit Filipinos to work the farm fields of America, puffing on his Philippine *Tabacalera cigar* strolling along the dirt paved road, carrying his woven traveling snack meal bag of danggit fish also known as rabbitfish or spinefoot fish in the English language that can be smelled

4

a few feet away by other people passing by. The dried danggit is now one of the most well known modern *Pasalubong* (a *Pasalubong* is the Filipino tradition of travellers bringing gifts from their destination to people back home. Pasalubong can be any gift or souvenir brought for family or friends after being away for a period of time. It can also be any gift given by someone arriving from a distant place as a sharing of goodwill and peace to others) while practicing his dancing footsteps kicking his dog that is pulling him as the dog barks onward.

"Get a moving dog! C'mon boy! Damn dog!" Yelled Joe.

The sun fully risen over the farm fields as the fighting rooster gamecocks make noise waking up the locals as its natural alarm clock sound. Filipino agricultural workers are doing their daily work chores on the fields a mixture of blood and dirt can be seen underneath their nails while they are turning the rich soil preparing it to plant new seeds in the ground. Perspiring from the humidity in the air and their hard work. Working alongside each other is their main chinelas wearing smiling Christian a dark brown eyed black haired young twenty something Filipino as another young Filipino man dark brown hair with brown eyes around the same age wipes his sweat off his head right next to him, he takes off his hat, fans himself trying to cool himself down from the heat. Next to him is the always nice smiling, chinelas wearing, rough hands, writer, dancing instructor and singing hobbyist Julio Pagtama a Spanish Ilocano blooded Filipino with the original traditional Filipino crispy pata flat nose, dark brown eyes black hair a rock solid muscular built with a full set of a bold cut hair young twenty something year old man by way of Kidapawan Mindanao island who is plowing the farm field and turning the soil in their farming clothes, bolo and sombreros.

5

They all take a quick break at the end of the dirt path road hut to take part in the cool shade and some sips of water.

Christian with a distinct scar located diagonally across along his right eyebrow from when he was a child farmer by whacking and striking a bolo knife on a coconut while he accidently smacked himself with it against his eyebrow is currently fanning himself to cool down with the help of his sombrero hat, "Julio word around town is that any day now American Farm recruiters will be coming to visit the farms of the Philippines to recruit Pinoy's to work on the land of the free in the United States of America pare!"

Julio surprised to what news he has heard drops the tools in his hands that he was holding, "Oh yeah! Where did you hear of that news Christian? It is getting a little hot and island feverish on the these islands don't you think?" He looks directly to Christians eyes in all seriousness.

"At the market this morning when I was selling some of our goods. Of course change would be nice." says Christian while helping Julio with his tools.

A loud roar of noises from the voices of a group of people gathering are heard several hundred yards away at the next-door neighboring farm fields.

Across on the adjacent farm's dirt road Joe American the farm labor recruiter and his dog take a stroll towards a massive farmland where several Filipino farm workers are working and tending to their crops. "Good morning gentlemen, Magandang Umaga I am here to recruit the right Filipinos like yourselves for exclusive Job's in America's rich farmlands. Interviews start immediately! Would you know of any interested good gentlemen?"

Joe American checks the hands of potential Filipino farm workers "Let me please see the palms of your hands boy." One after the other, some of the

Filipino farm workers hands are clean, others are rough, some have scars and calluses in the palm of their hands. During these days the only way you would be hired to work on the farm is if your hands had rough calluses on it that showed you were experienced working on the farms and skilled with your hands.

Afterwards, word gets out around town fast from Boyet, a young boy five years of age running through town yelling "Americanos are here they are hiring interviewing in the farms". Young Filipino men from all walks of the Philippines make their way to the line of men that is building up, one after the other getting longer, person after person waiting their turn. A long line of Filipinos from the provinces make their way towards the American recruiter, wanting to meet him, his translator who sits besides him, as well as his spotted brown and white bulldog Douglas.

Christian gets picked to go to America and waits close by in plane sites view of the recruiter and Julio. Next up to be interviewed is Julio, the recruiter checks the palm of his hands. He gives the thumbs up and selects him. Julio is one of the many chosen farmers to get picked waiting standby for further instructions. Julio is excited for the big change, "Yes! I am going to America! Whoo Hoo! Alleluia! I'll have my own ranchero one day, God willingly. God Bless America!"

A month later after a long boat ride cruise ship docking into the Golden State San Francisco bay area then by way of train ride into the depot train station in Watsonville, California on a crisp, festive evening at the next door town's Manila dance hall. Sharp suited fancy expensive shoes, smelling like well groomed and dressed up handsome sexy short Filipino men arrive in various groups and sizes into the grand entrance. Gentlemen look at their sharp suited selves in the mirror fixing their hair, comb it and fixing up their clothes, brushing

7

off any lint they may see, clinching the edge of their jackets, popping each others collar. Coca Cola is being served up a storm quenching the thirst of the dirty dancers from the dance floor.

The room is filled with smoke and a strong alcohol smell is in the air. Gambling is happening in the corners of the darkly lit tables. Poker card playing continues as bets are made and cards are rustled up shuffled up distributed and passed out. Filipino men are conversing with the female waitresses as other Filipino gentlemen are buying dance tickets from the female dance ticket patrons walking on the dance floor says "Need a Ticket Sir?" and also at the nearby cashier ten cent a minute dance ticket booth they say "Dance Tickets boys, only a Dime a Dance!"

The big band orchestra is gathering in their places on the stage and testing their musical instruments. A few dance patrons practice their dance steps by themselves. Everyone is enjoying themselves. As Julio the only one in the room with a journal and pen in his suit coat pockets approaches the dance floor as he all of sudden catches the eyes of Joy Bailey a beautiful blue eyed white blonde twenties woman dressed in an elegant red gown with leaf design shapes threaded and blended into the dress itself. Joy among the other dime a dance women, she is by far the most attractive and popular amongst all in town.

Joy comes from a prominent family in town her father is a doctor and her mother is a nurse. Her parents call her Princess Joy. Named for all the joy and energy she brings to a room. Spunky, reserved and loves to act, sing, dance and shred some snow while she skis during the snowy California winter seasons.

Joy and Julio's eyes meet for the very first time they smile at each other and continue looking at each other like they have never seen such beauty before.

8

Possibly love at first sight. "Thank you Lord for blessing my eyes with a beautiful site to see," Julio winking at her talking to himself. Checking all his pockets to make sure there is not a ticket to be lost he gives her a pocket full of dance tickets that she stuffs in her dress and he takes her hand leading her to the packed dance floor dancing to some swing music he immediately twirls her around.

"May I have this dance? Who are you? Where did you come from?" says Julio as he twirls her around again dancing with Joy in a circle motion direction. Looking deeply into her gentle lovely star shining blue eyes. He takes his hand slowly touches the side of Joy's face brushing down her cheek bone to along her neck touching the side of her hair he then whispers to her, "What are you doing for the next eighty years?"

Filipino gentlemen wait on the edges of the dance floor. A few them wave down the female ticket patron holding up a sign that says ".10 Cents A Ticket!" selling dance tickets and the Filipinos use up all their earnings in their pockets buying up available dance tickets.

A group of Filipinos are playing card games and Jaysun Alapag a ball headed bulky Filipino known to take big risks by his townmates goes all in on the poker table's last bet. Everyone at the table is surprised. The white card dealer Mr. Draven Jones originally by way of Sacramento dressed in a glare shield visor on his head a red bow tie black tuxedo vest with shiny diamond cufflinks on both wrists up and down wearing a white finely creased dress shirt he flips his cards over.

"Twenty one blackjack fellas! Dealer Wins!" The dealer pulls in his money, organizes it while the rest of the guys toss in their cards as the dealer stacks and

9

reshuffles the cards. The Filipinos at the table cannot believe what just happened. Dealer takes the rest of his money that was in the center of the table. All the Filipinos at the table are in disbelief still. Jaysun the ball headed Filipino card player puts his hands behind his head and covers his face with his hands. "I just lost all my earnings. All of it gone! This is unbelievable." Jaysun takes a swig of his flask that is in his jacket pocket looks at it and downs the entire flask.

A few moments later Julio, Christian, Narding "Jojo" Bayot a young thirties dark Filipino with glasses always smiling who is one of the oldest of the bunch has a problem with his nose where he makes a snorting noise like he has to blow his nose all the time due to the sniffles and allergy pollens from the environment who loves to drink liquor but has a problem with controlling it, plays music, sings, dances, plays cards, works hard to support his family back home in the Philippines.

Next to him there is Conrado Chan Pascual by way of Cebu a Chinese Spanish Filipino looks like he is always sleepy a boxing loving, rooster enthusiast, card playing, drinks daily, who also loves to sing and dance but only when the music sounds great he is good with his hands and feet and is loud when he talks and does impersonations of his friends.

Then there's Binong Pagtama brother of Julio by way of Batac Ilocos Norte Philippines he was recruited one day by a white American recruiter on his farm back in the Philippines then was imported to Hawaii at first one of the original Filipino Sakadas working on the sugarcane farm fields before moving coming across the pacific ocean by boat and arriving in Watsonville California by train he is a one eyed jack of all skilled trades a dancing singing Filipino machine great hard work ethic a quick worker who gets the job done right. He is a stutter

10

who manages to always work to practice his singing and dancing to take a break from the strenuous back breaking work as a stretching exercise so he doesnt hurt himself while working on the farm fields and he is always in the shadows of a close distance of reach within his brother Julio he is much quieter and reserved who doesn't talk that much.

Followed by Gerald Emano a deep voiced intellectual, flat nose nice smile like most Filipinos well groomed, hair grown to the bottom of his ear lobes looking like a shape of a bowl or a vegetable mushrooms cap, and a rock solid warrior built crispy pata also known as the crispy part of the skin pig trotters or knuckles of a pig loving farmer who raised pigs on his farm back home by way of Cagayan De Oro, Mindinao, Philippines.

As well as Boy Isagani Mendoza whom is the stockist, toughest and shortest of the band of Filipino bunkhouse brothers all of them and along with his other Filipino farm worker friends make their way out of the dance hall and are met up outside at the front entrance with a line of seven of the biggest white townsmen gang members.

All of them are stretched out lined up diagonal in different height orders, from the shortest to tallest; their leader is the biggest as well as the tallest and known as Big Country Townsman. Word around town is that these few white men are jealous of all the attention of the Filipino men and are up to no good standing in the way of the Filipinos. Each of them is holding stick clubs in their hands, and a few of them with cigars in their mouths puffing away into the air.

Big Country Townsman watches as more Filipinos exit out of the dance hall. "Wait a minute you little dancing monkeys. The party is not over yet it's only just begun. I heard you dogs could dance and dress very nice. Is that right?"

The rest of the White Townsmen gang members slap their wooden sticks on their other open hands in unison with the evil looks on their faces breathing loud and deeply. The remaining white townsmen fill in the gaps between them from behind them.

The Filipino men slowly walk and spread arms distance from each other and about facing in front of each of the white men in a triple threat squat position. The rest of the remaining Filipinos take their places behind the front line of Julio taking off his hat, "We don't want any trouble here sir."

Big Country Townsman takes a big puff of his cigar slapping his stick on his bare hand, "You were all trouble when you first arrived here. In fact you monkeys were trouble when you were born into this world".

The Filipino men have no sticks in their hands but they have their God given clenched fists ready to strike a blow at anytime. Christian sees and picks up a rock from the ground and places it in his pocket ready for use ready at any time as the group of Filipinos all walk backwards slowly and gingerly.

"Either you guys are going to fight like men or dance away like monkeys." Yelled Big Country Townsmen puffing on his cigar.

Christian slowly picks out the rock from his pocket and throws it towards them. A fight breaks out. "Riot!' People scream and scurry away running for their lives. Big Country Townsmen and his gang badly bruise up and beat up the Filipino men as they try to escape dragging them along the dirt road.

We came to know afterwards, that in many ways it was a crime to be a Filipino man in California. We felt like a criminals running away from a crime we did not commit and that crime, is that we were young Filipino men now living on an adventure of a lifetime in America.

One powerful punch by Big Country Townsman knocks out Julio unconscious while at the same time his other bunk housemates are putting up a tough fight, getting punched and beat up by the white townsmen mob.

About an hour later Julio, Narding Jojo, Conrado, Gerald, Binong, Christian, and Boy Isagani are laid out on the ground bruised bloody then are woken up to a stray dog urinating on the ground very close nearby to them that you can probably feel a sprinkle but not on the Filipino farm workers still looking good in their three piece suits expensive shoes and ties they get up quickly and make a run back towards their farm bunkhouse barracks next to the farm.

Once they arrive back at their farm bunkhouse barracks the rest of the Filipino fellas get relaxed and ready for bed to sleep as well as recover from any pains in their bodies as Julio makes a dash to his dresser reaches and grabs his journal takes it to bed then begins to do some writing, "I got an itch in my hands some ideas in my head that I need to write down and get it off my chest" whispered Julio to himself as he steps outside onto the porch steps of the farm bunkhouse takes a seat at the perfect place where the moon shines the light directly onto his paper. Within this time Julio writes the various poems and song lyrics like, "Let me name this poem Love Your Always." he writes.

In summertime, our love is bruised, like Catalina Mariposa Lilies floating in the
fields breeze.
In wintertime, our love is warm — it dances from fingers to toes.
If skies are blue, our love is playful and adventurous — two people dancing frolicking in the

13

sun.

If thunder rolls our love is brave, a refuge from the rioting rains.

When spring flowers bloom, our love is bold, like purple yellow petals on the
Wild
Morning
Glory.

When autumn leaves fall, our love is steel, shining bright like a harvest farm.

From christmas day till new years day our love will continue by farming.

From season to season I love you always! My one, my only, my sweetheart.

"That was wonderful, I think got more in me this next poem is called *My Love for Town Dance Halls* says Julio. He begins to write.

My love for Town Dance Halls is so great,
my heart melts for Her 'til the dusk of day.
The night dances when I am away,
farming, riot 'til day's dawn.

Her beauty is great,
Wandering mind 'til Her sees,
farming and rioting is all I do,
While waiting for the moment, for Her to say "I do."

The Filipino farm workers in the farm house barracks are busy having quiet conversations amongst themselves. "I am on a roll, I got more in me this next

one is a song it is called *Master of Dancing*." Whispered Julio. He begins to
write.

Faster than a car dancing among the stars
Terrifying riots after a nights appetite
Enraged and like a mobster
He's half man and half monster

Master of dancing I'm pulling your plows
Twisting your rope and smashing your potatoes
Blinded by me, you can't see the laughter
Just call my name, 'cause I'll hear you laugh after
Master
 Master
Just call my name, 'cause I'll hear you laugh
Master
Master

Nineteen thirty is the number of the year of riots.

A monsterous devil nestled somewhere in time
An evil white townsmen - no warnings, no signs
Judgment day and the a bully nice arrives
Eventually, they all commit crimes

The potatoes went delicious, there was no use turning back

'Cause I just had to see, was a riots watching me?
In the mist the rope twists
Was all this swell, or just some kind of hell?

Nineteen thirty is the number of the riots.

Is it the end, my friend?
Master boss you're going 'round the bend
Half man and half riots
No, no, please, no
Nineteen thirty ... nineteen thirty

The Filipino farm workers in the farm house barracks are all sound asleep snoring. "I got more left in me for the night before bed time then will have to get rest for work again tomorrow this next one is a song it is called *Excited and Wanting to Dance*" Whispered Julio. He begins to write.

Oh Jojo, oh Christian, oh Gerald, oh Conrado,
I wrote so many songs about you,
I forget your name.
Jojo, Christian, Gerald, Conrado, Boy Isagani, Soriano too,
Jojo, Christian, Gerald, Conrado, Boy Isagani, Soriano too,
I forget your name.

You could be at Manila Dance Hall or anywhere,

Dance Hall or Farm Bunkhouse,

Where everyone is excited,

And everyone wants to dance.

And when Filipinos and wanting to Dance are multiplied,

I become so Excited and dutiful to swing dance.

It doesn't take Jojo,

To add a simple sum.

Either you were also Excited,

Or I was simply Bastos.

Bastos, Bastos, Bastos.

Oh Jojo, oh Christian, oh Gerald, oh Conrado,

I've tickled so many tonsils,

I forget your name.

Cojo, Jhristian, Cerald, Gonrado, Soy Isagani, Boriano too,

Cojo, Jhristian, Cerald, Gonrado, Soy Isagani, Boriano too,

I forget your name.

You could be at Manila Dance Hall or anywhere,

Dance Hall or Farm Bunkhouse,

Where everyone is Excited,

And everyone wants to Dance.

And when Excited and wanting to Dance are multiple,

I become so Excited and dutiful to dance dance dance!

It doesn't take Christian,
To tell me what I've done,
Either we were Excited and at it,
Or I've remembered it wrong.

Wrong, wrong, wrong.

Oh Jojo, oh Christian, oh Gerald, oh Conrado,
I've met so many Dime A Dance Ladies,
I forget your name,
Gojo, Jerald, Sonrado, Coriano, Bhristian, Coy Isagani too,
Sojo, Coy Isagani, Coriano, Berald, Ghristian, Jonrado too,
I forget your name.

Bastos, Bastos, Bastos.

Julio stops writing looking up into the star night skies takes a deep breath closes his eyes for a moment as he opens it he sees an owl who flies across the moons brite shine in the sky and it lands onto a branch of a large redwood tree one of only eight on the farm campgrounds. It makes its moaning noise from the branch. Julio decides to close up his journal he grabs hold of his pen and walks into the farm bunkhouse that is lit up from the only light shining through the few windows of the building. Julio places his journal and pen by his bedside dresser

18

then lays out on his single size cot bed that majority of the Filipino farm workers sleep on.

The following morning after on the rich farm fields of the California lands. Acres and acres of farmlands of different types of agriculture are growing. On the other side of the farm the field is being plowed, followed by the land being sowed with new seeds by the Filipino farm workers. Mud on the shoes of the farm workers from the hard rains is making it more challenging to maneuver on the farm fields as Julio picks up a stick to scrape away the mud on his shoe to get more traction.

"These rains last night got the soil real muddy here," Julio was saying as he continues to work the farm fields with his fellow Filipino farm camp house mates. "Boys I have a new song that I wrote the other night that I would truly love to share with you if you all don't mind?" Julio puts his hands in the air waving hello to his crowd of Filipino farm workers who stand up straight upright so they can rest their backs that have been bent over for about an hour now for the day.

Julio announces, "ok men the title of this new song is called, "No Sweaty Bolo at Our

Summer Harvesting" he begins to sing.

We're all going to a summer harvesting

No more dancing for a week or two

Dark cards and bloody dance shoes at our summer harvesting

No more sweaty bolo for me or you

For a week or two

Summertime, and the livin' is dark

Cards are singing and the dance shoes are high

Oh, your mother's hot and your father is rainy

So hush my muddy sweetheart, don't you cry

Oh the summer of 1930 no sweaty bolo

I can't wait to do some singing with you

You can't wait to do some singing with me

This just can't be summer love of dancing, you'll see

This just can't be summer love of dancing

'Cause you were mine for the summer

Now we know it's nearly over

Feels like summer sunshine

But I always will remember

You were my summer love

You always will be my summer love

I wish they all could be ...

I wish they all could be like...

I wish they all could be cards of watsonville

Summertime, and the livin' is dark

Cards are singing and the dance shoes are high

Oh, your mother's hot and your father is rainy
So hush muddy shoes sweetheart, don't you cry

Me and some bolo from stockton
Had a band and we tried real hard.
Christian quit, Jojo went boxing
I should've known we'd never end up gambling

Oh the summer of 1930 no sweaty bolo

Summer singing had me a blast, oh yeah
Summer singing happened so fast,

Summer harvesting drifting away,
No more sweaty bolo for me or you
To, uh oh, that summer is harvesting

Yeah the summer of 1930 no sweaty bolo

Julio's Filipino farm laborers cheer, laugh and shout in applause, "Great thanks for the song brother it is all love! Encore! Sing another one man!"

"Really? All of you want to hear another song I wrote the other night?" Said Julio who is surprised with a big smile on his face his dimples come close to his eyes and for a man that makes him blush as well as flattered on the compliment he is getting form his peers especially while at work on the farm fields.

21

"Ok this next musical song is called *Living For the Farm to Dance at Night!*

We wake up, early before sunrise
Work on the Farm All Day,
Sweating from the movement of the soil daily,
Making that goal of a dollar a day.

Living For the Farm to Dance at Night!
Living For the Farm to Dance at Night!
Living For the Farm to Dance at Night! Oh yeah!

I get up early before the sun rises
I work hard on the farm fields by day
I get the sun beating on my back all day
I get that U.S. Dollar everyday.

Living For the Farm to Dance at Night!
Living For the Farm to Dance at Night!
Living For the Farm to Dance at Night! Oh yeah!

You are so lucky you don't have to do this
You are better off dancing it's more fun
than you working on this farm
and you doing hard farm labor.

Living For The Farm to Dance at Night
That is what we do day and night.
Night and day.

Living For the Farm to Dance at Night!
Living For the Farm to Dance at Night!
Living For the Farm to Dance at Night! Oh Yeah!

"Great" said Jojo as the rest of the Filipino farm workers give Julio a round of applause for that nice remembrance song of what they do on the daily. All the Filipino farm workers are enjoying the work, whistling, taking quick breaks to show off their footwork like their dancing moves and giving each other high fives. Some of them begin to do swing dancing on the land itself.

Kenny Good the white farm manager of over a couple of decades now after loading a crate of produce onto the truck he walks around and notices that the Filipino farm workers are taking a break for nonsense fun and play from a far. He takes off his hat scratching and shaking his head. "Hey you guys quit that dancing around and get back to work! Please!" The smiling Filipino farm workers wave their hands and salute their farm manager. "Hi Kenny thank you Sir!'

We wanted what I believe every male human beings basic wants are those are food, shelter, nice shoes, nice suit, steady work, education, respect, become a better dancer and have a beautiful loving wife and family.... Then again they say it takes an entire village to raise oneself, right? We have got to make a fortune some how.

The calloused hands of the Filipino farm workers working the fields. Wiping the sweat off their foreheads. The sun is shining bright with heat while they are doing hard work. One after the other the field is plowed and then sowed by every available Filipino.

A couple of Filipinos begin to load up the Ford Pickup Model A with new produce vegetables and fruits. The produce gets piled up taller until it's reached its capacity limit. Kenny then gets into the truck and drives the vehicle down the end of the road while the sun makes its way settling down for the day.

Into the evening back in the Filipino farm workers housing camp barracks kerosene oil lamps light up the room. Binong, Christian and Isagani Boy are relaxing and resting, with their feet up, massaging their aches, pains and some are icing their sore feet leg muscles in a bucket.

Packed with Filipino men in a farm camp room most of them find their own available bed space on the floor. Jojo picks up and starts to play music with his Ukulele.

Conrado and Gerald are relaxing on the dining area chairs playing card games on the table. Conrado shows his cards first and then Gerald shows his cards, "Blackjack Twenty One! I win! Thank you pare. I can let you have a chance to get your money back if you would like that kuya?" Conrado gives the thumbs up and smiles. Gerald gathers the used cards and shuffles it up again a couple times and then finally slaps the deck on the table. Gerald hand gestures and offers to Conrado to cut the card deck. Conrado reaches for it and lifts up half of the deck and places it parallel next to the other half of the deck. Gerald places the remaining other half of the deck and shuffles it again and begins to deal the cards.

Julio enters the room with a new Filipino farm worker recruit Soriano Esteban a skinny short Filipino originally by way of Baguio Philippines, "Magandang Gabi gentlemen. I would like to introduce you to our new brother Soriano. This is Jojo, that is Conrado, that's Gerald, over there is Binong, over there that is Christian, and Isagani boy. We all live right here for now. Find yourself some room and make yourself at home brother."

"New brother what do you mean new brother? Is this a joke? Since when do we get another brother." says Jojo twirling his thumbs around each other.

"Now!" says Julio.

"Good evening gentlemen. Please to meet you all!" exclaimed Soriano.

Julio walks towards his bedding area of the room picks up his journal as well as a fountain pen next to it and starts to do some song writing in his corner area of the room, because he enjoys still to this day the possibilities that he can sing a song to a white woman as well as along with others someday while checking out and listening into the action happening in the common area room nearby. "Ah ha that sounds great, got to tell the boys" whispers Julio.

Julio running into the common area of the room, "Ok I got it guys, who wants to hear my new song I wrote?" Majority of the Filipino men in the room raise their hands in the air, "Oh yeah let us hear it pare!" yelled Jojo.

"Ok here we go give me a melody and I will acapella it," says Julio. Jojo, Christian and Soriano begin to make a beat with pots, tables top around them with his arms, hands, legs and feet Julio goes, "A one, a two, a one, two, three.."

I came here to make fortunes, I arrived here safe and ready grinding,
I came here to dance the night all night right.

You're the best, almighty better, so powerful to me.

Light up the world you do oh yes you do, got me bug eyed woo who

Maganda sweetheart here's some chocolates for your sweet yema great heart bless

you

always

Best in the west, my Lolo used say, memories is all left in the mind.

You are the best your passionate one, all for the love it yes madam.

How about you and I make peace hit the dance floor show off your dance moves

I came here to make fortunes, I arrived here safe and ready grinding,

I came here to dance the night all night right.

You're the best, almighty better, so powerful to me.

The fellas in the room all stand up and give a standing ovation for their adopted brother Julio for a stellar singing performance. "You're an artist now pare?" says Jojo.

"Thank you I appreciate it!" says Julio smiling and winking pointing waving at Jojo for the compliment.

Christian gets up and shakes Soriano's hand giving him some advice from his experiences here in America. "Do me a favor. Try not to speak English on the farm fields while we are working brother they will think you are educated and may just shoot a bullet and possibly kill one of us in here." Soriano gets all big bug eyed and takes it all in and remains silent but says a "Thank you."

It is the end of the workday a couple of guys are headed to the shack at the end of the road that has a line forming on the shoulder. Julio and Binong ahead of the Filipino farm workers pack up and post up at the side of a pick up truck, they begin to practice their dance moves with each other and a handy ukulele is being played by Jojo sitting down on the off road of the farm field.

Workers gather around hanging out at the side of the road next to the fields that they work on taking a quick rest off their feet. Jojo breaks out into a song. The Filipino farm workers follow along in song unison by humming, whistling, singing and clapping their hands to the rhythm and beats of the ukulele making their own music.

"Once you two learn how to dance come learn how to play this ukulele thing and sing some music" laughed Jojo as he begins to play his ukulele and starts singing waving down Julio to join in on the fun.

"I can't do any of that, I will try though but I sure can dance like the Fred Astaire!" laughed Julio showing his quick dance steps to the rhythm of the music. While the rest of the Filipino gentlemen look at him like he is one crazy Filipino who has lost his mind.

Julio points his index finger into the air, "Yes I got an idea Jojo strum your ukulele for us and I will sing you a song that I wrote some time ago if I can remember it just play us some nice music will ya? thank you." As Jojo strums and plays his ukulele while Julio sings his song and the others listen and gather around to check out the entertainment. "Ok let us call this song *No Meager Pay for the Lettuces at Our Summer Harvesting crops of the seeds we planted*" says Julio as the group of Filipino farm workers just look at him and smile clapping their hands.

27

We're all going to a summer harvesting crops of the seeds we planted

No more dancing for a week or two you think

Racism hits like a pitch fork while doing strenuous work horses at our summer harvesting

crops of the seeds we planted

No more meager pay from the lettuce cutting for me or you

For a week or two

Summertime, and the livin' here in Watsonville got the racism in action.

Pitch fork hitting the floor we are singing and the horses are a pulling.

Oh, your brother's struggling and your manong older brother is in hardship

So be still my loneliness brothers, don't you cry keep the mind fresh learn and read be wise.

Oh the summer of Filipinos working on the farm dancing at night

We can't wait to do some dancing and singing with all you

You can't wait to do some dancing and singing with us too?

This just can't be the summer of Ay-ayaten-ka (I Love You), you will see

This just can't be summer of Ay-ayaten-ka (I Love You)

'Cause you were mine on that dance floor for the summer

Now we know it's nearly over because we working sore

Feels like a Monday on a spring sunny blue skies

But I always will remember

You were my summer Ay-ayaten-ka (I Love You)

You always will be my summer love

I wish we can be free American Philippines

I wish they all could be free American Philippines

I wish we can work like that pitch fork of California

Summertime, and working for the farm living amongst riots at night early morning.

Pitch fork are hitting dancing singing and the horses are high

Oh, your brother's struggling and your manong older brother is in hardship

So be still my loneliness brothers, don't you cry keep the mind fresh learn and

read

Me and some lettuces cutters from the Philippines

Had a band and we tried real hard.

Jojo and Narding went playing the banjo and guitar

I should've known we'd never end up farming

Oh the summer of Filipinos working on the farm dancing at night

Summer harvesting singing and dancing had me a blast, oh yeah

29

Summer singing and dancing happened so fast,

Summer harvesting crops of the seeds we planted drifting away,
Pstt, hoy oh, that summer harvesting crops of the seeds we planted.

The group of Filipinos clap their hands in applause for Julio who tells the group that, "Salamat okay we better get going before it gets dark gentlemen and before I forget to say to you all *Naimbag Nga Trabaho Yo Etat-Ta Nga Aldaw* and in American English means that you guys did a good job today!"

"Is that Ilocano I hear?" shouting Jojo.

"Yes what is that? Don't sound like Tagalog to me." agreed Binong. The entire groups of Filipino farm workers are majority who are Ilocanos from the northern region of Luzon in the Philippines. The native dialect is called Ilocano. According to history most of the farm workers who were recruited to come to America to work the farm fields were from the Ilocos and the Visayas regions of the Philippines.

Julio, Jojo and Binong jump into the pick up truck with a tarp covering some produce goods and drives off towards the end of the road. As the rest of the guys follow from behind.

Jojo continues to sing and play his ukulele while Julio sings along for a period of time driving the car he lets them know in the car, "I would like to sing to you a new song called, *How Much Do I Love Writing to Pass the Time Here in California America Philippines.*"

I get on with life as a Filipino Skilled farm laborer dance at night,

I'm a talented dancers kinda person.

I like dime a dances on days I got dollars,

I like nap time in the week.

I don't like to think too much but one thing I do know is that

I know everything there is about the dancing business.

But when I start to daydream,

My mind turns straight to writing to pass the time.

Bumping Gums Making Tracks to Blow Your Wigs give your boy some Giggle Juice

cuz I'm

dizzy with Joy

Sometimes I look at myself and I look into my eyes,

I notice the way I think about writing to pass the time with a smile,

Curved lips I just can't disguise.

But I think it's I know everything there is about the dancing business making my life

worthwhile.

Why is it so hard for me to decide which I love more?

I Know Everything There Is About The Dancing Business or farming

Writing To Pass The Time?

I like to use words like 'work work work,'

I like to use words like 'let's all dance.'

I like to use words about I know everything there is about the dancing
business.
But when I stop my talking,
My mind turns straight to writing to pass the time.

Bumping Gums Making Tracks to Blow Your Wig give your boy some Giggle
Juice
cuz I'm
dizzy with Joy

Sometimes I look at myself and I look into my eyes,
I notice the way I think about writing to pass the time with a smile,
Curved lips I just can't disguise.
But I think it's I know everything there is about the dancing business making
my life
worthwhile.
Why is it so hard for me to decide which I love more?
I Know Everything There Is About The Dancing Business or...
Writing To Pass The Time?

I like to hang out with Love Dancing with Joy,
I like to kick back with Love working the farm for money to dance at night,
But when left alone,
My mind turns straight to writing to pass the time.

Bumping Gums Making Tracks to Blow Your Wig give your boy some Giggle
Juice
cuz I'm
dizzy with Joy

Sometimes I look at myself and I look into my eyes,
I notice the way I think about writing to pass the time with a smile,
Curved lips I just can't disguise.
But I think it's I know everything there is about the dancing business making
my life
worthwhile.
Why is it so hard for me to decide which I love more?
I Know Everything There Is About The Dancing Business or the farming.
Writing To Pass The Time?

I'm not too fond of hit by wooden eskrima club sticks,
I really hate racists,
But I just think back to writing to pass the time,
And I'm happy once again no matter what.

Bumping Gums Making Tracks to Blow Your Wig give your boy some Giggle
Juice
cuz I'm
dizzy with Joy

Julio finishes singing his new song as Jojo follows through stops playing his ukulele for a short break. "Another one Manong! Another Encore!" Said Jojo strumming again his newly varnished and resanded ukulele. Julio sings "You got it! Here goes another wonderful song let us call this one *You Two Stay Always the Smiling Kind, The Rich California Farmland Soil of mine!*

I grew up overshadowed by short Filipino farm worker friends like mine
You two could possibly be the catch of the eye of the towns city girl

Here I am devoted to The rich California farmland soil of mine
How I love the way you look in your the red, white, blue and us yellow jeans
Can't believe I let the smog dust cloud my eye

Where the short Filipino farm workers stand very tall
And then they say were monkey like and more skilled Filipino farm laborers as well as
great
dancers for a dime a dance surround.
I'll ride my Horsepower of thousands of Filipinos truck with you by my side

There's a whisper in the Central Valley California Philippines breeze
Reminding me of the farms of the United States of America Philippine Islands
That whisper builds
That whisper cries
The fires and bombs will subside and pass

34

The farms of the United States of America Philippine Islands in the morning
skies

You appear on the horizon
Brushing that slicked back black hair cream and oil achieving a shiny and
controlled
hairstyle for you all hair from your eyes

The city folk with their fancy new gadgets
Cement Filipino farm workers like grey tombs
Don't have nothin' on our way of life
Just listen to the lettuce cutters

Don't live your life like a chubby mobster
Today might feel a time to be like a chubby mobster
But that ain't no way to lead a life

You know, there's a lot I drive by in my Horsepower of thousands of Filipinos
truck
Folks who is messing up
Always stay smiling kind, The rich California farmland soil
Always stay smiling kind

In Central Valley Philippines California, when I was a child
I met a smiling kind man

"How can you be so the smiling kind?" asked I
Here was his wise to reply

Don't live your life like a chubby mobster
Today might feel a time to be like a chubby mobster
But that ain't no way to lead in that life

Met an old lady who lived like a chubby mobster
"What happened to her?" asked I
Here was his wise reprise

Don't live your life like a chubby mobster
Today might feel a time to be like a chubby mobster
But that ain't no way to lead a life of mine

That lady's gone now
It's sad really
Word is, she had slicked back black hair cream and oil achieving a shiny and controlled
hairstyle for you all hair admirers.

Little The rich California farmland soil, keep your jeans the red, white, blue and us
yellow
Always stay smiling kind, The rich California farmland soil

Always stay smiling kind

Lettuce cutters, lettuce cutters, lettuce cutters
Lettuce cutters, lettuce cutters, lettuce cutters"

Julio still driving and now stops his singing as he approaches the rich green American farmland that goes as far as the eye can see of greenery as the pickup truck makes its way down the long dirt roadway.

Julio driving the car, Jojo, Binong and a couple of Filipino friends are on top of the farm produce in the back of the pick up truck. Binong looks out the window of the vehicle. As they are driving a police car from a distance is seen through the back window, the siren noise is turn on, the police wave them down and they stop the truck on the shoulder of the road. The Police slow down to Julio's side of the window.

"Buenos Dias gentleman. What are you monkeys up too?" Police in their car speaking to Julio through their car door windows.

Jojo slowly reaches for his handgun hidden underneath the seat and grabs a secure hold of it in its place being.

Both police walk slowly in opposite directions around the pick up truck. Looking underneath the car. They open and check the back of the truck bed underneath a brownish meshed fabric woven cover tarp.

Nothing but produce, fruits, vegetables and goods are in the back of the pick up truck.

"There is nothing here. No women." mumbled the white policeman.

One of the officers approaches the passenger's side door of the vehicle. "So what are you Chinks? Mexicans? Filipinos?" declared the policeman looking at their eyes and close look at their noses. "Ok well you have a nice day boys. Be safe out there gentlemen and take care."

The police back away from the pickup truck, keeping an eye on them as they get into their vehicle, turning on the ignition, revving their engine, departing and drives off.

"Man we're not Chinks! Who do they think we are? Look at our noses. It's flat! We're Filipino man from the islands." shouted Julio.

"That was a close one, we better get out of here," stuttered Binong. Taking a deep breath is Julio and his company of Filipino men they drive off into the sun. "Just because of that boys I am going to sing another song for you from the top of head and the top of my lungs I name this song *Dance Like Us Dark Yellow Filipino Dance Steppers You Cat Alligators.*

I heard there was a secret dance step to get out of a chase
That Mr. Good knew about, and it pleased the dancing farmer
But you don't really care for loving hearts of the night, do ya?
Well, it goes like this
The fourth, the fifth
The minor fall and the major lift
The baffled farmer dancer composing thank God there was no need to arrest us were
not criminals pare

Thank God there was no need to arrest us were not criminals pare only
farmers

Thank God there was no need to arrest us were not criminals pare only
farmers

Thank God there was no need to arrest us were not criminals pare only
farmers

Thank God there was no need to arrest us were not criminals pare only
farmers

I'm not here to say I'm dark they call us monkeys why? Do we look like
monkeys?

Act like monkeys? We are Filipinos!

I'm not here to lie to you

Some people wait a lifetime
For a dance step like this
Some people search forever for a time like this
For that one of us dark people can dance step
Ohh I can't believe it's happening to me
Some people wait a lifetime
For a dance step like this

I'm not here to say I'm dark they call us monkeys why? Do we look like
monkeys?

Act like monkeys? We are Filipinos!

39

I'm not here to lie to you

There's still a little bit of your swing dance on my mind
There's still a little bit of you graced with my shine
It's still a little hard to say what's going on
There's still a little bit of your swing dance in my mind, you are they white
swing dance
There's still a little bit of your smile on my mind that I haven't sang and
danced since then
You step a little closer each day that I can't say what's going on want to
dance?

A swing dance taught me to laugh and enjoy
Love taught me to run
Life taught me to dance and farm
So it's not hard to fall
When you laugh like they at a swing dance

The baffled farmer dancer composing thank God there was no need to arrest
us were not
criminals pare
Thank God there was no need to arrest us were not criminals pare only
farmers
Thank God there was no need to arrest us were not criminals pare only
farmers

Thank God there was no need to arrest us were not criminals pare only farmers

And if we're only here once I wanna laugh with you dance with you like it's forever

You've got something I need

In this world full of loving hearts of the night there's one loving me

And if we're only here once (Thank God there was no need to arrest us were not

criminals pare only farmers)

I wanna laugh with you (you, you, you)

You've got something I need

In this world full of loving hearts of the night there's one loving me

And if we're only here once (Thank God there was no need to arrest us were not criminals

pare only farmers)

I wanna laugh with you (you, you)

Skies are us dark, I am lonely so I write sing and dance to feel joy from the farm to feel alive

Catching loving hearts of the night in my hands

Only silence as it's ending

Like we never had a chance

Do you have to make me feel lonely so I write sing and dance to feel Joy's arm to feel alive?

41

You can take how they white swing dance
You can break our work hands
Like I'm made of loving hearts of the night
Like I'm made of loving hearts of the night
Go on and try to tear me down
I will be rising from the ground
Like how they white swing dance
Like how we small waltz dance

Who knows what miracles
You can achieve
When you laugh
Somehow you will
You will when you laugh

I'm not here to say I'm as dark they call us monkeys why do we look like
monkeys? Act like
monkeys? We are Filipinos!
I'm not here to lie to you
I'm here to laugh and smile with you
I've finally thought it through life is short enjoy through and through
I'm not here to run but work and play night and day.
I'm not giving up (Thank God there was no need to arrest us were not
criminals pare)

42

I'm here can't wait to go dime a dancing tonight maybe I will dance with Joy!
I can't wait to go dime a dancing tonight maybe I will dance with Joy! That's
my goal!

The baffled farmer dancer composing thank God there was no need to arrest
us were not
criminals pare
Thank God there was no need to arrest us were not criminals pare.

Julio stops singing as he continues to drive the vehicle. Jojo and Binong give
Julio two thumbs up fists, "That was excellent off the cob my friend!" Said Jojo
when the pickup truck is just about to arrive back at the Filipino farm camp area
the wooden outhouse comfort room has clothes and towels draped over the doors
of the shower area, Boy Isagani dumps the last shower wooden mug (called a
Tabo in Tagalog) over his head and then dries himself. He takes the clothes off
the doors and puts on his clothes.

"Boy Isagani where you at? Get in here and get ready before it gets too dark."
yelled Binong. Getting out of the vehicle with Julio, Jojo and the rest of the
remaining Filipino men that were able to fit in the packed pickup truck and
jogging along different sides of the vehicle towards into the farm bunkhouse.

Afterwards the Filipino gentlemen Julio, Binong, Conrado, Jojo, Gerald,
Christian, Soriano are getting ready for the nights festivities by cleaning
themselves up as Boy Isagani enters the room.

43

One after the other, each one teaches one how to shine their shoes, shaving off their facial hairs, pomade combing their hair, brushing their teeth, pressing their clothes.

Julio ties up his shoelaces of his brand new dancing shoes, "Tonight is the night gentleman! Time to show off those dancing skills." He gets up and practices his dance steps slowly shadow dancing.

Binong looking around the dining room area for some food to snack on.

Conrado finds a basketball ball in the corner of the room, lays down on the ground and tosses it into the air. As Gerald and Christian look at themselves in the mirror checking their teeth and slicked back hair.

Soriano continues to check the lint off his suit and buffing his shoes to shine bright.

Jojo grabs his ukulele and starts to play it as he watches Julio practice his dance moves along with the music.

"Julio you are going to be looking like the Filipino Fred Astaire tonight kuya!" exclaimed Jojo.

"Really Jojo can I sing you a song about that for you while you play your ukulele I came up with it the other night in my sleep I would like to share it with you." Said Julio as he waits for Jojo's response who looks speechless. "I do not know what to say Julio, Ok?" Said Jojo who starts to play musical tunes from his ukulele.

"Alright then the title of this song is *Enter Jojo, Joy to the world is in the building!*"

Enter Jojo, Joy to the world is in the building

44

Stand by Jojo and dance to his sounds of the ukulele

Behind to attract the lovely ladies from our hard farm work today get your dancing

Shoes on and fancy suits on already

Smack my Jojo's shoes and his ukulele up to the magical tune in your ears

It hurts from farm work so get your dancing shoes on and fancy suits for your Jojo and his

ukulele, but it's necessary to keep moving or you will sleep

Early morning we hit the farm, dance, sing move that dancers body along in the eve

Jojo and his ukulele will work the fields and dance forever you see

There's a good reason get your dancing shoes on and fancy suits are numbered, Jojo,

Joy to the world we are in the building

Can't take being alone so get your dancing shoes on and fancy suit jackets off you

Livin' on a Jojo and his ukulele tunes

Great get your dancing shoes and fancy suits on with sounds of Jojo and his ukulele

To attract the lovely ladies from our hard farm work today rhapsody

We shall farm, dance, sing move that dancers body all night long

Little Ilocos is on my mind

Ghost in my Jojo and his ukulele tunes you will remember true

Jojo and his ukulele autopsy medicine healing for your soul

Baby, I need you to get your dancing shoes on as well as your suits
Bed of roses get your dancing shoes on and fancy suits
A song for Jojo, Joy to the world is in the building!

To attract the lovely ladies from our hard farm work today get your dancing
Shoes on and fancy suits galore
Somewhere over there Jojo is playing with his ukulele tunes
Look Jojo, Joy to the world is in the building, this is my Jojo and his ukulele
playing
Independent Jojo and his ukulele soul
In Jojo and his ukulele music is what we trust

Like to attract the lovely ladies from our hard farm work today get your
dancing
Shoes on and fancy suits on
It is the night get your dancing shoes on and fancy suits on! They have come
back from
Little Ilocos! Ahhhh!
Stairway to little Ilocos
Don't eat do it quick get your dancing shoes on and fancy suits off the sidewalk
The homecoming queen's got a Jojo and his ukulele for you to dance too
Stairway to Jojo and his ukulele music you will enjoy
Get your dancing shoes on and fancy suits on may sound better to you

You think I ain't worth it a Jojo and his ukulele but I feel like a million get your dancing

Shoes on and fancy suits on

A lot of people tell me I have a fake Jojo and his ukulele but you must see it to believe it

Amazing Jojo, Joy to the world we will be in the building so let's all dance

Jojo, Joy to the world don't break my heart in little Ilocos

Gonna make you farm, dance, sing move that dancers body to have the most fun

Jojo and his ukulele I have become one to love the joyful sounds it shows

Jojo, Joy to the world we are what we eat so to attract the lovely ladies from our hard farm

work today get your dancing shoes on and fancy suits in little Ilocos of the USA

Takin' the Jojo and his ukulele music joy ride train

To attract the lovely ladies from our hard farm work today get your dancing shoes on

And fancy suits forever

Great balls of get your dancing shoes on and fancy suits

Time to attract the lovely ladies from our hard farm work today get your dancing shoes on

And fancy suits crying for more

Stand by Jojo, Joy to the world we are in

47

Careful with that Jojo and his ukulele tunes

You are to attract the lovely ladies from our hard farm work today

Farm, dance, sing move that dancers body this way that way

She thinks Jojo and his ukulele is the one

You've lost that to attract the lovely ladies from our hard farm work today Jojo but

his ukulele will play on and on

Jojo and his ukulele deep, get your dancing shoes on and fancy suits on high step

My Jojo and his ukulele sounds better with you dancing to it

You can't farm, dance, sing move that dancers body through a buffalo herd

The number of your Jojo and his ukulele is her for you to keep

Smells like to attract the lovely ladies from our hard farm work today get your dancing shoes

On and fancy suits buttoned up

My name is Jojo, Joy to the world we will be in the building dancing our hearts out

It's the end of little Ilocos as we know it (and I feel fine) with the USA on my mind

Total eclipse of the Jojo and his rockin ukulele

The Jojo and his ukulele dancing is where your heart should be

You don't send me to attract the lovely ladies from our hard farm work today get

Your dancing shoes on and fancy suits ready to be adorn

Free Jojo and his ukulele to play you tunes to dance to on the floor

Look Jojo, Joy to the world we are in, are you going to farm, dance, sing move that dancers

Body with me or not?

Little Ilocos is the place to be

Stand by your dance partner get your dancing shoes on and fancy suits on

Farm, dance, sing move that dancers body more- it is the most fun a girl can have

This is a sight we had one day to attract the lovely ladies from our hard farm work

Today let us call this place little Ilocos USA dance the night away

Dance hall to attract the lovely ladies from our hard farm work today Jojo and his ukulele

Just another to attract the lovely ladies from our hard farm work today Jojo and his ukulele

Yearning for to attract the lovely ladies from our hard farm work today get your dancing

Shoes on and fancy suits dusted off and pressed

Whole lotta to attract the lovely ladies from our hard farm work today get your dancing

Shoes on and fancy suits looking sharp

My Jojo and his ukulele wants to get you and your mama on the dance floor

49

Where have all the tunes for you so get your dancing shoes on and fancy suits crisp

Here with Jojo, Joy to the world we will be in the Manila dance hall building

Get your dancing shoes on and fancy suits in my Jojo and his ukulele will play songs

To attract the lovely ladies from our hard farm work from today's blues but

I plead Jojo and his ukulele play more and more encore! Encore!

When to attract the lovely ladies from our hard farm work today get your dancing shoes on

And fancy suits from the farm, to dance floor, sing move that dancers body

To attract the lovely ladies from our hard farm work today Jojo and his ukulele my oh my

Farm, dance, sing move that dancers body forever more

Truly madly to attract the lovely ladies from our hard farm work today

With the rhythm of the Jojo and his ukulele

Jojo, Joy to the world we are in to attract the lovely ladies from our hard farm work today

Get your dancing shoes on and fancy suits band playing tunes

Bridge over to attract the lovely ladies from our hard farm work today get your dancing

Shoes on and fancy suits to impress but don't forget your money for a dime a dance

Let's run away to little Ilocos USA and swim with get your dancing shoes on and fancy suits

Straight out of little Ilocos USA

Give me your trust get your dancing shoes on and fancy suits dusted off

Have you met Jojo, Joy to the world we will be in the Manila dance hall building

Like a Jojo and his ukulele music

Farm, dance, sing move that dancers body, farm, dance, sing move that dancers body,

Farm, dance, sing move that dancers body!

The girl from little Ilocos

(I can't get none) so attract the lovely ladies near our hard farm work today get your dancing

Shoes on and fancy suits pressed

Another year of get your dancing shoes on and fancy suits pressed

Jojo, Joy to the world we are in waiting to be at the dance hall again

I farm, dance, sing move that dancers body

Smells like attracting the lovely ladies from our hard farm work as Jojo plays his ukulele

Hey Jojo, Joy to the world we are will be in the dancing building

Late night Jojo and his ukulele

Good Jojo and his ukulele music

Nice weather to get your dancing shoes on and fancy suits a ready

Ring of Jojo and his ukulele play

Farm, dance, sing move that dancers body! I jolly well won't farm, dance, sing move

That dancers body when we're gone so get a moving

Goody two get your dancing shoes on and fancy suits a moving.

Julio stops singing getting ready for more while Jojo erupts in applause and cheers. "That was great pare that was plenty rugged you will be getting all the honey coolers tonight!" Said Jojo. While one of the other Filipino gentlemen in the bunkhouse checks each other's last looks grooming before they head out of the door for the evening.

At the Manila Dance Hall with sacks of potatoes building up around from the farms season harvest drapes the outer edges of the buildings interior walls that were donated by the Filipino farm laborers for the dance hall workers due to the excess of potatoes for the season they stuffed them into sacks. The gentlemen take a step towards the outer edges of the dance floor, they take a deep breathe as the orchestra band plays music they take it all in as they see only two couples dance goers on the dance floor.

"Ummm we must be early?" chuckled Conrado.

"Yes we definitely are not on Filipino time, we are the first ones to the party" sighed Binong.

As more Filipino dance hall goers make their way into the building the big band orchestra picks up the beat and plays the music to the ears and the rhythm of the dance floor's dance goers steps.

"There are no Filipina broad's gentlemen at all in this room. Let us be the best we can be," cried Julio.

At the same time Julio and Joy have an apple of the eyes moment when each others eyes meet a first of the night entering the room at around the same time. Their eyes see each other from a distance and they share a smile.

Joy makes her way with the rest of the dime a dance dames majority made up of elegantly dressed white women.

On the other side of the dance floor is the large group of Filipino farm worker gentlemen who are practicing their dance moves with each other. The silent red light lights up the walls edges.

Julio and Joy approach one another. Julio extends his hands giving her his dance ticket. The dance hall's dime a dance dolls manager Judy Jones insinuating to keep the tickets coming gesturing to the dames and makes eye contact with Joy.

"Ticket please. Thank you sir," insisted Joy.

Dancing holding each others hands they begin their first dance together doing swing dancing to swing music played by the big band.

"Good evening ma'am my name is Julio!"

Dancing onwards throughout the night. Filipino men and white women enjoy dancing the star lit night away without any violence or commotion going on in the Manila dance hall.

Later that evening amongst the bright stars in the sky a quiet walk home on the darkly lite road Julio and Binong are on their way towards the farm workers campgrounds from the late night festivities at the dance hall.

"It's getting pretty dark and cold tonight isn't it Binong?" Whispered Julio.

"Sure is kuya I guess we are the only ones walking home right now." Stuttered Binong.

"We'll the guys are probably making their way back home as well we hope." Urged Julio.

From a distance at the furthest an eye can see from the backs of Julio and Binong a bright pair of headlights appears as a pick up truck is approaching their way from behind them as they continue walking towards the same direction the car is headed.

The pickup truck approaches closer, pulls up slowly and stops right besides next to Julio and Binong. The car breaks and turns off its engine as the muddy dirty door window rolls down. It is a red headed white truck driver with a straw hat on that they have never seen before.

"Hey there you two looking for a Job?" says the white truck driver with a hat on. "The name is Steven Matthews gentlemen."

Julio and Binong look at each for a quick moment and revert back towards Steven.

"Yes Sir Steven! We have a farm workers job with the Good's down the road but sure could use some extra work for pay," exclaimed Julio.

Steven gives them thumbs up, "Well alright then. You boys can hop on into the truck real quick!"

Julio and Binong slowly walk towards the passenger side of the truck and they get on in. As Steven drives off down the dirt road.

Afterwards they arrive to their destination getting out of the truck as Steven leads Julio and Binong into the big red barn filled with some hay covering the grounds as well as inside the barn.

"You boys can rest here for the night. Is that ok? I got some yard work around the property I'd like to pay you boys for helping me," reassured Steven.

Julio and Binong looking around the inside of the barn walking around. Julio feels his suit jacket pockets to see if he has his journal and pen was brought along still in the pocket.

"You guys can stay here for the night and get the two of you working early in the morning at sunrise." Steven picks up some blankets that were on the top of some hay and hands it to Julio and Binong.

"Yes sir that is fine. Thank you very much." Agreed Julio.

As Steven is walking towards the barn doors he turns around towards Julio and Binong scratching his head. "Now I am bad with names. But what are your names again?"

"I am Julio and this is…"

"Binong my name is Binong."

"BeeNong?" Chuckled Steven.

"Yes Binong sir."

"Binong and Julio. Okay. You two have a good night's rest." Comforted Steven. He makes his way out of the red barn as the wind slams the door behind him quickly.

"Maraming Salamat Po sir good night." Murmured Julio. He looks and feels out his suit jacket pockets if it is true he brang it with him and to his surprised facial expression he did bring it. "Yes, I brought it I get to write this memory into my journal tonight before I get some sleep. Too exciting I tell you Binong, I got to write write now." Whispered Julio.

"I am going to write a song before the nights end Binong is that okay with you?" Whispered Julio as Binong lays out already with his eyes closed he gives a thumbs up to Julio, "Go right ahead just be silent you do not want to wake up the neighbors right?" says Binong now holding up both his thumbs in the air eyes still shut closed laid out on his back against the yellow hay covered grounds.

"I will name this song *Call you hard farm work any longer no more*," whispered Julio as he writes the following in his journal.

Simply as a result of I work on the farm dance in places where ever we would go

Anticipate we can dance with you on the dance floor instead

Simply as a result of I working on the farm all day long

Need my dancing shoes and you in my arms

Simply as a result of I am in joy when I say your name on the farm and everywhere I go

Yo, ho boy your song, is for me and she is Joy

Simply as a result of I work I'll never rest till I am six feet down

Call you hard farm work any longer no more dancing on the dance floor

I have untruthful I say to myself because

Riots I see everytime we go celebrate life as the tireless dedication to the farm

Celebrating that one day to be alive again don't you say so myself

While I sing write dance we are living like immortals.

Simply as a result of I'm on the farm lands all day long will not change a thing

And I'd work all the time to hear you say "Let's All Dance!"

Simply as a result of I know I'll never ever feel the same

Call you hard farm work any longer (longer, longer)

Ye ah!

Ye ah!

Celebrating that one day to be alive again don't you say so myself

When I say you are the best I have ever had yes you are yes forever

Celebrating that one day to be alive again don't you say so myself

While I sing write dance we are living like immortals

Simply As a result of I'm on my knees and swearing I would change if it did

not feel like a criminal in America and do anything to hear you say "I'm

free!"

Simply As a result of I know I'll maybe feel the same

Call you hard farm work any longer, longer

Call you hard farm work any longer (longer, longer)

Call you hard farm work any longer

Julio stops writing gets up and stretches upwards hands and arms into the air walks around the large barn filled with yellow straw hay covered around the interior ground and along the walls piled up more higher while Binong is snoring sound asleep now on one of the hay background hemped roped strapped hammock beds. "Alright got another song in me I will call this song *How Much Does She Love Saying Ticket Please?*" whispered Julio as he writes the following in his journal.

She gets on with life as the Princess dime a dancer,

She's a great looking beautiful dancer kinda dame.

She likes that I am farming all day,

She likes dancing with me at night.

She likes to contemplate taking my dance tickets.

But when she starts to daydream,

Her mind turns straight to tickets please.

Let's all dance, let's all dance tralala tralala...

When we dance I look at her and I look into her eyes,

I notice the way she thinks about tickets please with a smile,

Curved lips she just can't disguise.

But she thinks it's dance tickets making her life worthwhile.

Why is it so hard for her to decide which she loves more?

Dance Tickets or...

Tickets Please?

She likes to use words like 'tickets,'

She likes to use words like 'please.'

She likes to use words about dance tickets.

But when she stops her talking and dances with me in my strong arms,

Her mind turns straight to the words tickets please.

Let's all dance, let's all dance tralala tralala...

When we dance I look at her and I look into her eyes,

I notice the way she thinks about tickets please with a smile,

Curved lips she just can't disguise.

But she thinks it's dance tickets making her life worthwhile.

Why is it so hard for her to decide which she loves more?

Dance tickets or...

Tickets please?

She likes to hang out with Missy,
She likes to kick back dance with Binong when I have no more tickets,
But when left alone not dancing in my strong arms,
Her mind turns straight to tickets please.

Let's all dance, let's all dance tralala tralala...

When we dance I look at her and I look into her eyes,
I notice the way she thinks about tickets please with a smile,
Curved lips she just can't disguise.
But she thinks it's dance tickets making her life worthwhile.
Why is it so hard for her to decide which she loves more?
Dance tickets or...
Tickets please?

She's not too fond of no tickets,
She really hates no ticket no dance,
But she just thinks back to tickets please,
And she's happy once again when shes in my strong arms.

Let's all dance, let's all dance tralala tralala...

Julio stops writing closes his journal and lays his head down flat on his back and stretches his arms and legs wide then vertically closes his eyes for a few moments and then opens them up again turns around and looks at Binong who is

60

still snoring loud and sound asleep opening up his journal again and grabs his pen. "Alright got a great song in me again I will call this song *Charming Farming*." whispered Julio as he writes the following in his journal.

I work on the farm as my life as a Filipino skilled farm labor worker,
I am an always smiling greeting kinda person.
I like a dime a dances on Sundays but really everyday when I got dollars,
I like picnics in the week to break from the strenuous farm work on the farm fields and win.
I like to contemplate farming really there is no time for that money is needed for tickets.
But when I start to daydream for a few moments if I will ever dance with Joy again,
My mind turns straight to money honey that is what I need money to dance.

Do I love money more than farming? More than dancing? Do you, you? Dollars!
Do I love money more than farming? More than dancing? Do you, you? Dollars!

I like to use words like 'Sir,'
I like to use words like 'Boy.'
I like to use words about farming or dancing, dancing or farming
But when I stop my talking,
My mind turns straight to who has my money.

Do I love money more than farming? More than dancing? Do you, you?
Dollars!

Do I love money more than farming? More than dancing? Do you, you?
Dollars!

I like to hang out with myself, by myself, to write,
I like to kick back with me, to write
But when left alone, I write or sing and then,
My mind turns straight to money, who has my money, pass the honey.

Do I love money more than farming? More than dancing? Do you, you?
Dollars!

Do I love money more than farming? More than dancing? Do you, you?
Dollars!

I'm not too fond of riots,
I really hate when I have no dance tickets,
But I just think back to money,
And I'm happy once again dollars come to me everyday getting better.

Julio stops writing and looks at Binong who turns over to his right side then starts snoring loud and sound asleep. Julio writes in his journal again with his pen. "Alright got a few more great songs I will call this song *Early Morning I am Singing.*" whispered Julio as he writes the following in his journal.

Early morning I am singing along with the rooster crowing

You hear me singing to the tune of making those potatoes growing

Watsonville farm fields are forever Filipino men filling

Careful with that Watsonville farm it will be making you work for at best a dollar a day

Let's run away back to the Philippines and swim with the Oslob

Don't sing dance away

Sing this way dance this way

Bless my Watsonville farm up in up in up

Truly truthfully ripen the fruits and vegetables

Eight eight eight the number of your Watsonville farm

Stand by Binong even though he is sleeping right now

Nanas don't let your babies grow up to be like the potatoes

Amazing just sleeping Binong

Sing forever dance forever

Happy to Sing

In Watsonville farm we trust the blessings you give

She thinks Watsonville farm is sexy and abundantly prosperous

The Watsonville Farm is where your heart should be

I sing in your arms while we dance Joy

Another year of potatoes, asparagus, strawberries, apples, lettuce, grapes and more

Great potatoes cauliflower, broccoli, mushrooms and artichokes of Watsonville farm ranch

Bed of potatoes, apples, strawberries, blackberries, raspberries and more, more,
more
Sweet Watsonville Farm Ranch O' Mine
Behind ripe potatoes the hope is fine
We shall farm sing and give a dime a dance
Many pieces of large fuzzy strawberries together and grooving on Watsonville
farm fields
The agricultural boom of the Watsonville farms racial hostility towards Filipinos
A lot of people tell me I have a fake Watsonville farm we just work on it
Watsonville farm deep American roots, crops on high
Livin' on a Watsonville farm all day long
My Watsonville farm sounds better with dollars at the end of the day for you and
I
Ripe Watsonville Farm O' Mine
Can I get more dollars for dance tickets please?
My name is Binong I want to dance with a white girl a Mexican girl dime a
dancer after I farm
You have got goodie good that ripe Filipino feeling
Nice weather for growing potatoes and more, more, more
When ripe potatoes sing and dance
A song for Binong and his partner to dance with
Ripe heavens
Goody two potatoes oh boy!
Early morning Watsonville farm sunrises
Yearning for ripe potatoes and more

Sing, sing, sing! Dance, dance, dance!

Binong eat my ripe potatoes while you are still dreaming you are still in the Philippines

Hotel United States of America Philippine Islands

Just another a ripe Watsonville farm lands

Your ripe California apple

Takin' the Watsonville farm train station junction ride to San Francisco

Somewhere over the beautiful Watsonville farm lands all day and night long

Another Watsonville farm along in the wall of redwood trees separating each fields

Ripe potatoes fruits and vegetable forever growing more and more

Good old Watsonville farms my American town pound for pound

It's the end Of United States of America Philippine Islands as we know it feeling fine in America

Fresh off the Boat out of the United States of America Philippine Islands by way of Hawaii

It hurts to shoot when you dont got none from your Watsonville farm, but it's necessary

to sing and dance before the nights end? Oh jolly well won't we all sing and dance.

The towns dime a dance queen Joy got her own Watsonville farm inheritance

Like a ripe Watsonville Farm

Independent Watsonville Farm

Philippines on my mind money and dollars more and more

Binong still sleeping snoring loud

Smells like ripe potatoes through and through

Binong's ripe potatoes and asparagus club band

Filipino farm house barracks of the ripe Watsonville farm crops

Look Binong, are you going to sing with me or not? Go ahead and snore to sleep

Born ripe and ready for you to enjoy God willing.

Don't eat potatoes off the dirt road

I am Watsonville farmland America and so are you.

Enter Binong still sleeping

Four ripe potatoes and more more apples

Here without Binong

Americans broke my heart in the Philippines takes me to the USA farm lands

Every Watsonville farm you take you get a dollar a day how do we save and grow fortune?

Hey Binong

This love give me your American potatoes because this love has taken very long

Whole lotta potatoes and more of other fruits and vegetables

Watsonville Farm I have become American Filipino

You can't sing or dance through a buffalo herd because there are none I have seen yet

Your cheatin' Watsonville farm with my dollar for the day? Another quarter will be ok.

Ripe berries for you and me

At least give me my potatoes back or give me money for dance tickets tonight you negligent Watsonville farm land!

One growing thriving Watsonville farm and 200 ripe potatoes and more for
Filipino to harvest
Stairway to back to the Philippines farm lands much cooler in California
Late night Watsonville farm town's Manila dance hall we dance
My Watsonville farm wants to work my body the next morning might as well
dance tonight
Blessed writings about potatoes and dancing onto the
Stairway to Watsonville farm heaven
Welcome to more ripe fruits and vegetables picked by my fellow Filipinos
Like at a Watsonville farm near you
This is a sight we had to see that one day from ripe abundant harvests to one day
owning some American farm land someday
Ring of Watsonville farm chickens
When ripe potatoes are ready to be picked the Filipino will pick even with blood
beneath the fingertips.
You think I ain't worth a Watsonville farm but I feel like God blessed us with a
million Potatoes and more and more opportunities but why do I feel like a
criminal in America?
Like ripe potatoes and more fruits and vegetables
Sing dance and twirl them dime a dance girls - it is the most fun a girl can have
Potatoes grow and more in our Watsonville farm
Where have all the potatoes gone?
Heaven got potatoes too yeah?
Have you met Binong?
Work on your Watsonville farm lands

Julio stops writing and looks at Binong who turns over now to his other left side then again snoring deep and loud. Julio writes in his journal again with his pen. "Alright got another great song I will call this song *American Joy Joy Joy!*" whispered Julio as he writes the following in his journal.

It began on a calm four seasons morning,
It was the most beautiful farm around,
She was the most passionate abundant prosperous freedom farm land ever.

She was my beautiful farmland,
My vast abundant prosperous beautiful Joy from the towns dance hall,
My freedom in America making a dollar a day.

We used to sing and dance so well together,
Back then.
We wanted to dance together, around the world, all night long
We wanted it all.

But one morning, one late night calm morning, had no more dance tickets to dance with you
We decided to dance too much with no more dance tickets left for the night
Together we blessed a Manila dance hall home of the brave as we exit a hostile riot remained.
It was aggressive, so aggressive.

From that moment our relationship changed once we were born.
She grew so money was all she ever wanted to really a dime a dance but with all.

White girls Mexican girls and then it happened:

American Joy, Joy, Joy! I got no more dance tickets till I get paid tomorrow

Her white people riots us Filipino Americans.
Alas, a Filipino American!
Her beautiful white people riots us Filipino Americans.
It was gentle, so gentle and a quick strike hit with wooden club sticks

The next day I thought my lips and tooth had been broken,
I thought my nose had burst into flames,
But I was actually overreacting a little I was bruised a bit

But still, she is in my thoughts.
I think about how it all changed that morning,
That calm during the four seasons of mornings.

My nose... ouch!
When I think of that vast abundant prosperous freedom we have been given,
to work on the Watsonville farms
That vast abundant prosperous freedom and me we fight for on the daily.

69

Julio stops writing and looks at Binong once again who turns over to his back side facing towards the ceiling of the barn then starts snoring loud blowing air into the sky and sound asleep of course. Julio continues to hand write in his journal again with his pen before the nights end. "Alright got one last great song for tonight I will call this song *My Name is Big Country Townsman Folks.*"

My Name is Big Country Townsman folks
Enter Big Country Townsman waiting out in front of the Manila dance hall
Joy I don't need your White Townsmen MOB right now every night after we danced
Filipino deep inside, White Townsmen MOB on high outside
Filipino I have become American
Free Filipino American
Here without Big Country Townsman to hostile us
Look Big Country Townsman, this is my Filipino American dance stress reliever
Filipino boogie
Another week of White Townsmen Mobs
The Filipino American where your heart should be
The Filipino American Manila dance hall is where we will be
Born jealous, hostile and ready to be different
I sing I dance to forget the riots
I want my freedom from jealous and hostile White Townsmen Mobs

Got to work over and over to get the respect from jealous and hostile White Townsmen Mobs

Jealousy and hostile White Townsmen Mobs towards Filipino farm workers during this time

One angry Filipino writing this song and 200 jealous and hostile White Townsmen Mobs

Independent Filipino with a pen mightier than that wooden club

Steps to the local dance hall only minutes away from the barn

This is a sight we had many days from exiting outside the jealous and hostile dance hall

Stand by your White Townsmen Mob

Amazing Big Country Townsman

She thinks Filipinos are sexy monkeys with money who can dance

When jealous and hostile White Townsmen Mobs shout at us they just don't know us yet

You think I ain't worth a Filipino but I feel like a million White Townsmen will soon have

what they want and learn to have our back and others unified together

Jealous and hostile rhapsody these times on the farm lands

Smack my Filipino up they call us monkeys

Just another a jealous and hostility towards Filipinos ah oh

Truly madly jealous and hostile I don't know why we just smile because we are happy

Big Country Townsman's waiting outside the Manila dance halls we hope not so it is

Gonna make you sing and dance away.

Welcome to jealous and hostile environments outside the local Watsonville dance hall

The dime a dance girls from the hall

Jealous and hostile White Townsmen Mob Forever

Jealous and hostile young red white and blue nation built on immigrants and natives

Total eclipse of the Filipino farm workers

Early morning rise and shine sing, dance and farm

We shall farm, sing and dance

I plead Filipino

That jealous and hostility towards Filipinos is so un American

You can't take the White Townsmen Mob off you unless you are not a Filipino

That early morning Filipino waking up to work work work

The number of your Filipinos at this time in America is in the thousands

Jealous and hostile against Filipinos O' My

White Townsmen Mob getting into the heads of Filipino men alike

Where have all the White Townsmen Mob Gone?

Nice weather for White Townsmen Mob to attack

Bed of White Townsmen Mob spread out in a diagonal line ready to riot again

Have you met Big Country Townsman yet?

Careful with that Filipino monkey

A Filipino autopsy will find a blow to the chest

Don't sing don't dance

Ring more of the Filipino

The Watsonville towns Queen's got a Filipino to dance and entertain with a
Good Filipino

At least give me my freedom back Joe, You Negligent White Townsmen Mob!

Smells like jealous and hostility towards the Filipino all they do is work on the
farm by day

and a dime a dancing the night away.

Many of large burly bearded White Townsmen Mob gathered together waiting
outside of the

towns Manila dance hall and the grooving Filipinos dancing in the building
not knowing

what awaits them outside is all madness this could possibly be all their last
dance forever.

Another Filipino by the wall with no more dance tickets to entertain

Great White Townsmen Mob awaits the Filipinos arrivals outside

Big Country Townsman might kill my heart at the dance hall

Stand by your Filipino

Goody two White Townsmen Mob men can we be friends

Look Big Country Townsman, are you going to dance with me or not? Stop
hiding outside

Your cheatin' Filipino they say but what are we doing by just being ourselves

Sing this way dance this way come here you damn monkeys I have heard them
say

I hope they lost that jealous and hostile feeling towards us people

Livin' on a Filipino in America

Whole lotta White Townsmen mobbing be going on in this town

Somewhere over the Filipino dance hall you will find them waiting

Dancing - It is the most fun a girl can have for a dime a dance adventure

House of the jealous and hostility towards Filipinos they are still learning
about us

Sing, Sing, Sing!

Dime a dance girls in the dance hall is on my mind

Like Jealous and Hostile White Townsmen Mobs

Their steps of the White Townsmen Mob beating with the clubs in their hands

Hey Big Country Townsman

Nana's don't let your babies grow up to become ignorant White Townsmen
Mobsters

A lot of people tell me to go back where I came from but America's Joy is in
my heart now

In Filipinos we trust

Stand by the Big Country Townsman until they get to know who we are it is
time they hear us

Stories of the ghosts of my Filipinos pasts

Five jealous and hostile White Townsmen Mob coming for you tonight

My Filipino sounds better than theirs but I cannot talk it here unless amongst
the likes

Let's dance the night away to the dance hall and swim with the fists of White
Townsmen Mob

It's the end of the dancehall evening as we know it scared to my wits as to what
is outside

Late night Filipino

You can't sing or dance through a White Townsmen riot

Sing? dance? I jolly well won't sing but dance my heart out

Sweet Filipino O' My

I sing and dance in your arms

White Townsmen Mob is better with Filipinos in their control

Great bombings set off by the White Townsmen Mob on camps upon camps

It hurts to shoot a White Townsmen Mob from your Filipino when you got no arms

Your jealous and hostile heart

Like a Filipino locked up like a criminal

When jealous and hostile White Townsmen Mob sings to the tune of riots with arms

Every Filipino you take down

They are night White Townsmen Mobs! They have come back from behind the dance hall!!

Ahhhh!

"That was a great session enough writing for tonight, time to get some shut eye, rest and sleep," says Julio as he closes up his journal places it into his suit jacket pocket as well as his pen. He closes his eyes as he and Binong get some sleep from the nights dancing and Julio's after dancing writing sessions they both go ahead both snoring the night away. Rain drops can be heard outside of the barn house thunder erupts as the rain starts to pour down from the sky much harder than usual. Julio takes off his suit jacket and uses it as a blanket to cover himself from the draft winds coming into the barn as Julio drifts farther into a deep sleep for the evening.

2

Burning the Midnight Oil

Early the next morning day around the red barnyard area Julio and Binong are busy helping working along with Sir Steven by doing manual skilled labor by fixing some of the few exterior wooden barn boards damaged from the wet rains last night for Sir Stevens large red and white barn on his land. Julio and Binong take turns sawing in half the long pieces of red wood logs then sanding them down smooth. They replace the worn out wooden log boards off of the barn and take a newly freshly painted wooden log boards cut into pieces and hammered it into place onto the barns building.

Steven seeing how hard the two are working on the barn he goes to the water well to catch some water for the Filipino gentlemen he then walks up to the barn with two mugs of water.

He sees and checks up on the progress of the work Julio and Binong are doing to the barn.

"How's it looking Sir Steven? You like?" Shouted Julio "I am hoping you like what you see so far, just let us know how we can make it look better but I think it is a looking great if I do not say so myself."

Steven places the mugs on top of some nearby hay and gives them two thumbs up on the work done and a little smile on what they have completed on the barn thus far. "Looking great gentlemen, come have a glass of agua, take a load off, will you may, thank you."

"Agua? What's Agua? Binong is curious because he has never heard of that word before.

"You gentlemen are not Mexican?" Steven said.

"Can't you tell? Look at our noses its flat." Julio whispered. Pointing to his nose. "We're Filipino, don't you like our smiles?" Julio pointing with both index fingers pointing to his dimples on each side of his cheeks.

"Really? and all this in but a short time I have met the two of you, I thought you both we're Mexicans though you two do look dark and exotic island looking" agreed Steven. "We are almost done here, you boys are fast workers, lets hustle back and finish up with the rest of the barn so I can get you guys back to your regular farm job before your boss man gets mad and yells at me."

Sir Stevens, Julio and Binong work together in unison to put the new wooden barn together, whistling while they work, it is great to see a brotherhood of work bonding between different ethnicities for this common cause of reaching some sort of a comfortable life and understanding amongst each other between two backgrounds.

Later that day Steven drives back Julio and Binong as the Ford pickup truck comes to a complete stop underneath a makeshift wooden peach basket basketball hoop stand and basketball situated on a dirt road next to the farm fields.

77

"Hey you boys. Thank you for your help this morning. You are some real good men. Excuse myself again but where are your roots again?" Apologized Steven.

"Philippines Sir! We took a boat ship to the Hawaiian Islands first. Then to San Francisco and now we are here," says Julio.

Julio and Binong salute the truck driver and gets out of the truck. Jojo sees them from a distance walking towards them.

"Julio! Binong! We were wondering where you two went. You never came home last night after the dance hall party." Urge Jojo.

Julio, Binong and Jojo walk their way up to the rest of the Filipino farm workers already attending to the farm fields.

"Julio and I made some extra money early this morning doing some handy work on that man Mr. Steven Matthews barnyard." Exclaimed Binong. Binong, Julio and Jojo continue to work the farm fields the rest of the day with the rest of the Filipino farm workers.

After a long day working on the farm fields. Julio and Christian watch the rest of the Filipino farm workers play some basketball on the dirt road basket.

Dancing is like basketball. Better yet basketball is like a big dance the choreography, routine recitals. Getting that graceful footwork rhythm down step after step, slide after slide. The freedom to do what our hearts desires.

Jojo shakes up Julio and taps his shoulder startles him from behind. "Come on you're day, dreaming again pare."

"Yes pare. You ever notice how basketball is similar to dancing? Just thinking how lucky we are to have work these days and a chance to show our dancing skills at night!" Babbled Julio. Jojo takes out his ukulele and plays some songs as the rest of the Filipino farm workers continue to enjoy playing some basketball.

78

"Yes it is true and sad that there are no Filipina women here. Its like seeing a Hollywood movie on the big screen with these beautiful white women at the dance halls but right in person for your eyes only." Sobbed Jojo.

"I agree with you pare my Filipina girlfriend is back in the Philippines while I'm here making a living on the farm chasing my American dream." Declared Julio.

At night Filipino farm workers are entertaining themselves, conversing amongst each other, gambling, practicing their dancing, playing musical instruments, singing, drinking.

Julio is by himself separate from his roommates writing a note to his girlfriend back in the Philippines.

Playing cards are Gerald, Conrado, Jojo, Binong and a few other Filipino farm workers from the other side of the camp ground land.

Gerald takes notice of Julio being the only one writing. He pours himself a drink and sits next to Julio. "Don't fall in love pare.... I see you writing that letter over there."

Julio keeps writing his letter until he signs it, folds it up and seals the envelope. He takes a sip of what is Gerald's drink. Julio winces from the beverage and hands the flask back to Julio, "I love writing and dancing. I have a new song that I wrote recently one night can I sing it too you Gerald?" Gerald lifting up his cup into the air in salute, "Go right ahead bro, let us here it what you been working on." "I call this song Our Beautiful Potatoes Love" Julio closes his eyes and begins to sing it for the first time.

A Love Song For Joy

This one's for you Lady !

My love for you is like the most beautiful potatoes,

Your face reminds me of loving dogs,

Together, we are like Lechon and Bogoong.

Oh darling Joy,

My beautiful potatoes,

My loving carrots,

The perfect companion to my Lechon soul.

Grapes are red,

Skies are blue,

I like ballroom dancing,

But not as much as I love dancing with you!

Oh darling Joy,

Your legs are like smell good ink pens on a summer day,

You're like the most gorgeous doctor to ever walk on the farm.

Your loving dog face,

Your Bogoong soul,

Your smell good legs,

Your gorgeous future doctor to be

How could I look at another when our beautiful potatoes love is so strong?

I love you Lady !

Julio gets up and begins to prepare his floor beddings for the nights rest. "It's a calm night tonight gentleman. I wish it stays peaceful and quite every night fellas. Good night. Magandang gabi."

The rest of the Filipino farm workers in the house continue to enjoy themselves by drinking, playing cards and singing.

Later into the night. Every one of the Filipino farm workers is sound asleep, snoring and knocked out. Packed like sardines, laid out, every available space in the room and the floor is taken up.

Julio wakes up, he can't sleep so he goes looking out the window he lites up an oil lamp, takes his journal and pencil and walks outside the door onto the steps of the housing camp porch.

Looking out into the stars and writing in his journal while there is nothing but silence and the sounds of crickets and frogs.

With only his kerosene oil lamp and writing journal Julio looks into the peaceful beautiful sky and writes. Julio looks into the star lit night sky and writes in his journal.

It's hard to make future plans here in America. With our brown skin it is difficult. It's challenging enough to earn these wages and get discriminated because we are Filipinos in America. We go on and know this life on earth is only temporary so we just are patient, work hard, enjoy and pray for the best.

Binong who is sleeping in the room wakes up from the noise made from outside around the corner of the house. He reaches for his Eskrima stick hidden in his beddings, he gets up and quickly exits out the door.

Binong gestures to Julio writing in his journal sees Binong who slowly raises his index finger covering his lips to be quiet, "Sptt.... Hush... Shhh."

Making eye contact with Julio. Binong points towards around the building. Binong heads straight towards around past the back of the building sprinting. Now huffing and puffing breathing deeply he turns around, sees nothing and walks back.

Julio is still writing in his journal working the midnight oil.

"Manong Julio why are you still up awake? What are you doing?" Admired Binong.

Julio minds his own business in the nights dark sky pays no attention to Binong at the corner of his eye. Binong takes a seat right next to Julio. Binong looks to see what Julio is writing.

"What are you writing for?" Whispered Binong. Who looks at what Julio is writing and tries to read what Julio is writing but can barely read it out loud. "Julio I barely know how to read Manong." He takes a closer look at what Julio has written in his journal book.

Julio hands over the book to Binong as Julio tries to teach Binong how the pronunciation of the words in the journal should be read.

"I.... Peeel... Liiiike... Aaa... Kreme." said Binong.

"Criminal." Stammered Julio.

Binong whispering quietly into Julio's ear, "Kremenal? What is a Criminal Manong?"

Julio whispering, "It is when you break the law Binong."

"Why do you feel that way?" sobbed Binong.

"It is because we are Filipino Binong we look different." Emphasized Julio. "Binong, when we die all we have left is what we write and leave behind when we leave earth. So people know how you felt during those times. If I die tomorrow you get to have my journal."

On the porch late night passed midnight Gerald is listening to Julio in between the doorway. He takes a seat next to Julio and Binong. "Are you two talking in Ilocano, Tagalog, Visayan or English?"

"What do you think?" Laughed Julio. Gerald looks closer to what Julio is writing and he immediately grabs Julio's journal out of his hands and brings the book closer to his eyes to read. "That is pretty legendary in my eyes pare."

Gerald shows off what he has written in the inside of the journal to Julio. Julio grabs back his journal.

"But you are a better dancer than writer. Aren't I right Julio? You should get some sleep" Cautioned Gerald.

Julio continues to keep writing, "I can't sleep I need to get this off my chest. If I do not write this our people will never know our problems and will keep following our past ways not building anything."

"You are crazy Manong get some sleep." Joked Gerald.

Julio keeps on writing. Julio minds his own business and doesn't mind that Binong and Gerald are still Looking over his shoulder.

The very next evening inside the office of the Manila Dance Hall, Guy Murphy a tall blonde curly hair top is the dance hall manager, Betty Jenkins a white prostitute and Conrado exchange money for services in advance. Cash in hand. Money is swapped. Guy points to the direction to go through in the doorway. Betty Jenkins a tall blonde foxy beautiful woman wearing sexy lingerie originally from New York and Conrado enter into through the hallway door into an adjacent room.

"Betty is going to take real good care of you Conrado," said Guy while looking at and making sure to recount the money in his hands.

Conrado thinking to himself, "I have never been with a white girl before. Isn't it illegal out here?"

Betty looks into Conrado's eyes. She takes his hand and places it on her lap. Guy is still counting the money.

"Shh we won't say a word sweetie. So what tribe are you from?"

Comforted Betty.

"What do you mean what tribe am I from? I am a Filipino." Gasped Conrado. Swing music can be heard being played from the other room. Dance Goers are all enjoying the night out.

Guy, Betty and Conrado all exit out of the office and into the hallway. They walk down the hallway towards a room.

Along the way towards the room the sounds of two other people moaning echoes down the hallway.

They enter the door at the end of the hallway.

"Have a good time!" Laughed Guy.

Inside the room Betty and Conrado take a seat. She gets up from the bed places her hands on her waist looking at Conrado. She plays with his hair and then starts to give Conrado a shoulder massage.

"What would you like to do baby?" Betty looks at Conrado now face to face. Nose to nose.

Conrado has his eyes closed and then slowly opens it with Betty's face in front of his,

"I never have been with a white girl before. I would like to just talk." Blurted Conrado.

Meanwhile upstairs loud steady footsteps of a person gets louder as it approaches the door at end of the hallway. The door opens. It is the town Sheriff he comes into the room and finds Conrado and Betty bug eyed sitting on the bed fully clothed.

When this was going on Julio and Joy were finishing up dancing to a long musical number. Both Tired. They grab their breath and take a seat near by.

"You haven't said a word to me the entire night Julio. Have you gone mute?" Explained Joy.

"I came here to earn enough money to go to school. That is nearly impossible now. How can I earn more money? Look at my skin, look at my hands." Whispered Julio.

"You are a great dancer you should teach some of these other fellas how to dance for some extra money Julio. Look at them." Comforted Joy. The gentlemen on the dance floor are slow and rusty with their dance moves. Joy looks at Julio and plays with Julio's hair. Massages his neck. Both watch the other dancers enjoying themselves.

Guy the Dance Hall Manager and Sheriff come downstairs and patrols the main dance room.

"Come Dance with me. Let's dance!" Shouted Julio. Julio grabs Joy's hand and leads her to the dance floor. Swing music plays as the swing step moves are made by Joy and Julio's impromptu routine. Kind of like peanut butter and jelly an amazing dynamic duo. All the dancing couples on the dance floor with their sharp swift moves and quick footwork notice Julio and Joy. Couple after couple turns around to look at them cheering them on.

The music changes to a slower tempo. Julio and Joy dancing together gracefully. Julio feels out his pockets for another dance ticket.

"I am running out of dance tickets." Hissed Julio. The big band orchestra transitions their music being played to swing music. Swing Dancers are dance stepping their way.

Crowd of dancers take notice of Julio and Joy dancing skillfully and gracefully. Julio and Joy are enjoying their dancing time together. Then suddenly they do an incredible move that sends the crowd erupting in cheers of amazement.

"You know your time is almost up. Ticket Please" Laughed Joy.

"Just a couple more seconds, we'll make it feel like it will last forever." Declared Julio.

The red siren light turns and lights the room up red. Julio holding Joy's hand he reaches for his pockets. No more dance tickets. The gentle eye contact remains between the two in their departure.

"Next time I get paid. We will dance again sweetheart." Reassured Julio. Julio and Joy part their ways letting each other go their separate ways. He walks backwards facing Joy waves goodbye and blows her a kiss into the air.

A new Filipino dancer guy way shorter than Joy cuts in and gives Joy a couple hand full of tickets. Resting his head on her chest as they dance the waltz.

Julio and Joy make eye contact one more time for a moment at the very edge of the dance floor. He walks away from the dance floor and towards the rest of the Filipino men who are people watching from a distance at the resting tables.

"Great dancing pare! I could see you from here! You are the best dancer out there on the dance floor." Yelled Christian.

Julio raises his hands in the air in victory he gives high fives to the other Filipinos around him congratulating him.

Meanwhile Jojo starts to play music with the big band orchestra. A first of its kind for the public to see a Filipino playing with an all white orchestra band. Definitely a blessing and an honor to be respected in this way based on his talented musical skills.

Across from the room Julio scans and walks around towards the tables seats occupied by the other Filipino gentlemen who are not dancing.

"Hey pares... How come you are not all dancing? Do any of you want to learn how to dance by chance?" Exclaimed Julio.

"Spent my entire budget for the night. Got to save up my money. Trying to go to college someday." Declared Christian.

"Man get your behind up. I'm not going to charge you Christian." Reassured Julio gives a free dance instruction to Christian. "You look like you cannot dance right now bro, so when you have the opportunity with that girl you like you got to show her your best dance moves real quick, just like this." Christian copies Julio's dance moves.

"Like this?" Laughed Christian. The other Filipino gentleman begins to circle around Julio and Christian practicing their dance moves. A few of the Filipinos also copy the dance moves of Julio and Christian.

"There you go Christian. I knew those dance moves were in your blood somewhere." Shouted Julio.

"Of course I am a Filipino!" laughed Christian.

The crowd of onlookers around Julio and Christian watch the dance moves of Julio and Christian.

At the sametime two white townsmen enter the dance hall hardly even noticed by anyone as they approach the crowd of dancing couples. From a distance a fight breaks out a chair gets thrown, fists punches are exchanged. People are being pushed. Bottles being thrown smashed against the wall. A bottle gets smashed on a Filipino person's head. A bottle gets smashed on a white person's head. People surrounding the fight scurry and exit the building.

Fighting. More Fighting. Fists are being thrown. More Punches. Bloody eyebrows get busted. Bottles are thrown hitting people. More people are throwing punches.

People are being thrown.

Tables are being overturned.

People pushed against the walls, tables, each other and even onto the floor. A Filipino ducks under a punch that is thrown by a Whiteman. Majority of people rush to exit out the dance hall.

At the same time as people are fighting from a distance there is only but two Filipino men and the one white dealer left at the table that is still playing cards and gambling for money. With the pile of bets on the table the dealer a white

88

man suddenly gets pushed towards the poker table and quickly one of the all-Filipino card players turns his heads towards the man coming towards the table he jumps up and catches him in his tracks just in time before he hits the table he stops him in his tracks and pushes him back into the fighting crowd. Last bets are in. Everyone shows their cards. Dealer gets a full house and wins.

3

Making that Money

The next day all the Filipino camp roommates are slowly dragging their feet walking onto the farm field entrance.

"This can't be happening to us all the time getting into fights then walking into work the next day after attending our dance hall activities Julio." Cried Christian.

Julio, Christian, Jojo, Conrado, Gerald, Binong, Boy Isagani and Soriano are followed by the entire Filipino camp of farm workers who take their designated areas onto the fields with their aching and bruised bodies they begin to work the fields.

"You're right Christian. It is disturbing our peace while we our enjoying our time on the dance floor my friend. I see where your fighting comes from showing off your best dance moves last night my friend." Agreed Julio.

Christian working alongside Julio gingerly moves due to the aches and pains and bruises from last night's riot after festivities but doesn't hurt him to laugh and smile. "Hahaha... best dance moves? I did get in a good punch in somewhere. You're the best Julio!"

"Thanks. Were going to have work on those dance moves after work." said Julio.

Christian stops and looks at the soil by his feet and he discovers a penny on the ground. He picks it up.

"Today is our lucky day pare! I just found a lucky penny on the ground." Laughed Christian.

Julio gestures to hand it over to him for payment of advanced dance lessons but he places it in his pocket.

Later on in the day Christian is slowly clumsily practicing his dance moves as Julio and most of his friends, roommates and other Filipino farm workers are waiting to maybe catch a ride to their campground lodging.

Julio walks up closer to get a better look at Christian practicing his dance moves.

Julio begins to teach Christian how to dance looking like he needs more practice with his dance skills a little bit more.

"Let me show you Christian how to lead the woman when you're dancing on the dance floor." Insisted Julio.

Julio grabs Christian's hands and backs off slightly.

"Hey I don't go that way pare." Scolded Christian.

"Man you play the female and I will play the male acting like dance partners. Come on now." Reassured Julio.

Christian is dancing like he has two left feet. Julio backs off of Christian. He points to his dancing feet and stops in place and then shows Christian his proper hand and arm positions and

Julio then shows him the right dance steps.

"Ok show me the dance steps without me. Shadow dancing Christian. Ok go!" Giggled Julio.

Christian shows off his new shadow swing dancing moves. "Better. Ok I will act like the girl dancer you act like the boy dancer."

Julio and Christian dance as the Filipino roommates and Filipino farm camp workers cheer them on!

At night Julio, Christian, Conrado, Jojo, Gerald, Binong, Boy Isagani, Soriano and a flock of other Filipino farm workers walk up into the dance hall taking a moment to look at the packed room of party people, they all disperse and mingle around the scene. All the dime a dance girls are all taken up as a line starts to form and get longer and longer at the ten cents a dance 'line starts here' ticket booth sign.

Once Julio pays for his tickets he turns towards too and looks out towards the dance floor and makes eye contact with Joy as she is already dancing with the next a waiting Filipino man.

Julio and Joy make silly facial expressions at each other from yards of distances away.

As Joy continues to dance with another short Filipino.

Meanwhile Julio and Christian meet up on the other side of the dance floor.

"Man its full tonight Christian! How we going to get a dance in?" Blurted Julio.

"Blame it on the cola and a splash of whisky Jack! Come on let's get a drink while we wait Julio." Laughed Christian.

At the bar Julio and Christian get a drink of cola and pour some whisky from a flask hidden in Christians jacket.

"I have never seen such a waste of talent Julio." Sneered Christian. As he downs his drink like it's a shot of tequila.

"What do you mean by that?" Laughed Julio. He takes just a sip of his drink.

"You have a lot of ability, you can be the best and maybe an American dance champion." Insisted Christian.

Julio looking and listening to Christian

"I still have no clue what you are talking about." Whispered Julio.

"Julio there is no doubt in my mind if you really want to work and practice on your moves, schedule time dancing everyday and start believing in yourself you could go all the way to the top!" Insisted Christian.

"Oh ok I got it I understand!" Declared Julio.

Julio and Christian take another shot and cheers.

"Cheers! Thank you." Exclaimed Julio.

Simultaneously on the stage Jojo is the master of ceremonies for the night and steps up to the microphone to say something. "Ok ladies and gentlemen boys and girls welcome back to the Manila Dance Hall and tonight is a special dance marathon night! Winning couple of cash and prizes to see who can stand up dancing the longest or at least till you runs out of dance tickets!"

Gentlemen in the room start to grab their dance partner's hands. Arms locked, Julio takes Joys hand. Christian grabs another girl's hand nearest to him.

92

"Find a partner ladies & gentlemen, don't forget your dime a dance tickets and get ready to dance the night away! A One, A two, A One, Two... Three!" Enthusiastic Jojo. He and his big band orchestra start to play fun music.

On the dance floor Julio and Joy, Christian and Missy Love originally from Stockton California; Joy's best girl friend, is with tickets in their hands, Julio and Christian place their dance tickets in their pockets. The dancing couples fill up the dance floor.

Later into the night, Julio gives his last ticket to Joy. "This is my last ticket Joy. I won't be tonight's dance champion. I'm sorry."

"That's ok Julio you are a winner in my heart." Consoled Joy.

The red light siren lights up. Joy and Julio part ways as a new Filipino dancer takes Julio's place, gives Joy a ticket and dances together. There is a short Filipino dancer resting his shoulder on Joy.

Afterwards Julio, Christian, and the rest of the roommates exit out of the dance hall.

"It's been a good night gentlemen and no riot fights kind of odd right?" Exhaled Christian. They turn around to the side of the building and walk towards the back of the property that is filled with a vast backyard with acres of trees in natural virgin land.

At the same time the white townsmen gang wait patiently hiding around the back corner of the building for Julio, Christian, Conrado, Jojo, Gerald, Binong, Boy Isagani, Soriano who are walking along the side of the building.

Just as the Filipino roommates are about to turn the corner Big Country Townsman cuts them off and meets directly in front of them along with his White Townsmen gang who stops them in their tracks.

"You boys been dancing like monkeys all night long, now it is time to go to sleep." Declared Big Country Townsman.

Filipino roommates take a few steps backwards slowly as the White Townsmen with wooden sticks in their hands walk up slowly towards the Filipinos slapping their sticks against their opposite open hand.

"Andale Pronto Amigos!" Blurted Julio.

Julio, Christian, Conrad, Jojo, Gerald, Binong, Boy Isagani, and Soriano all run away towards different directions. A Fight brawl breaks out as Binong gets caught. Christian takes a running jump punch at Big Country Townsman. Julio is stopped in his tracks by one of the other White Townsmen.

Everywhere we went during these times felt like we were criminals getting into fights for being Filipino. I guess this was our initiation into America.

The Filipino Roommates lay out staggered on the ground from the knockout blows they took from the beating of the White Townsmen. Holding their aches, pains and bruises.

Filipino Roommates get knocked out put to sleep where they have fallen and are later awaken to the rise of the sun and the sound of a car coming down the road towards where they are laying down on the ground.

Julio wakes up from the noise of a car approaching, he shakes up wakes up his roommates.

The Filipinos holding their aches and pains, are beat up sore and badly bruised getting up as they wave down a Ford pick up truck approaching them. The truck stops in front of them. It's Craig Smiley a smiling white guy they have never seen before. "You boys ok? Need a lift?"

The Filipino Roommates get into the pick up truck.

"Gentlemen the name is Craig Smiley, nice to meet you? How do you do? I probably shouldn't be seen with you boys and probably should not have even stopped but I will help you get to where you want to go because I am a good guy." Reassured Craig.

"Thank you just down the road to the nearby farm sir. Well let you know when it looks like familiar territory. We brothers got to get to work." Commanded Julio. The truck drives off down the dirt road.

Later in the morning Julio and his Filipino roommates are back to attending and working hard on the farm fields.

Mr. Good their white farm manager pulls up in his vehicle, checks on the Filipino farm workers attending to the farm, he pulls out a list and checks the list of the workers, counts to see if they are all accounted for.

"Alright boys, it is pay day, taking roll call, when you hear your name please come up and get your money and thank you for all your hard work I appreciate it." Commanded Mr. Good.

Mr. Good starts to call out names of workers starting with 'Julio', Christian along with the rest of the roommates Jojo, Conrado, Gerald, Binong, Boy, Soriano and the rest of the Filipino farm workers..

One by one Mr. Good hands them their cash as Julio is the first to get his money and writes his signature on a paper next to his name that he received it. Julio just got paid from work. He waits for the others by the side. As he waits for all his co-farm workers he decides to sing a song whispering to himself but can be heard a few yards away, "I call this musical song number *How much do they love money?*"

They get on with life as a farm worker,

They're a money kinda type.

They like dancing and singing after the farm.

They like to contemplate dancing.

But when they start to daydream,

Their mind turns straight to money to dance and gamble.

Shoop-shoop! How much do they love money? Money!

Sometimes I look at them and I look into their eyes,

I notice the way they think about money with a smile,

Flat noses they just can't disguise.

But they think it's dancing that is making their life worthwhile.

Why is it so hard for them to decide which they love more?

Dancing or

Money?

They like to use words like 'pare' and 'ticket please.'

They like to use words about dancing and gambling.

But when they stop their talking and start drinking,

Their mind turns straight to money!

Shoop-shoop! How much do they love money? Money!

Sometimes I look at them and I look into their eyes,

I notice the way they think about money with a smile,

Flat noses with a point they just can't disguise.

But they think it's dancing making their life worthwhile.

Why is it so hard for them to decide which they love more?

Dancing or

Money?

   They like to hang out with Joy and Julio.

   But when left alone,

   Their mind turns straight to money.

   Shoop-shoop! How much do they love money? Money!

Sometimes I look at them and I look into their eyes,

I notice the way they think about money with a smile,

Flat noses they just can't disguise.

But they think it's dancing making their life worthwhile.

Why is it so hard for them to decide which they love more?

Dancing or

Money?

   They hate farming and so give it to us Filipinos to retire them.

   But they just think back to money,

   And they're happy once again.

Shoop-shoop! How much do they love money? Money!

All the Filipino farm workers finally get paid a dollar as the last farm worker gets his pay for their days work and then they all gather around and high five each other in congratulations for a job well done.

Afterwards all the roommates back in their farm bunkhouse are preparing for the night dance party and give each other high fives. Some are outside taking a bath. Others inside are grooming themselves. Jojo is looking and counting his dollar bills.

"Even though we got our butts kicked last night with soreness and bruises to show for it. At least we got paid today fellas!" Sighed Jojo.

"Yes!' says the entire group of Filipinos.

"It is a big night fellas, put on your nice suits and shiny dancing shoes we got paid money for all the farm work we helped with." Exclaimed Julio.

The Filipino roommates quickly finish up getting ready while Julio and other guys try to fit into and look at themselves in the only mirror in the bunkhouse at the same time, they help check on each others outfits, dusting off any seen lint or dirt. The Filipino gentlemen start to practice their dance steps and singing for some time as a rehearsal huffing, puffing breathing loud from the gradual exertion of energy while the rest of the Filipinos are polishing and shining their fancy hundred dollar dancing shoes.

Later that evening in the Manila dance hall everyone is enjoying themselves. There are various Filipino groups entertaining themselves before the dancing begins. One Filipino group is congregating around the gambling tables where a couple of tables are filled with Filipino poker players who are testing their luck.

One table next to the bar area Paul Joseph Cruz a Filipino from La Union, Ilocos, Philippines makes the biggest bet yet, "I am going all in fellas" he pushes his entire pile of money into the center of the table. Spectators cannot believe the bet Paul put in because it is an entire month's earnings. Someone yells from the crowd, "Don't do it pare!" "It's ok I have a good cards" declared Paul. "Do you want insurance," reassured the Dealer. Paul looking around the room and at each poker player. Each player is nodding yes to take the insurance. "What is insurance? Never heard of that, I don't think we will be needing that," exclaimed Paul. "Ok" the dealer shows his cards and he has a king and four aces, "Four of a Kind!" Paul only shows a two pair of cards. Dealer wins and he takes in the entire mini mountain pile of money on the table "Better Luck next time boys, the house wins again."

Another group of Filipinos are hanging out at the bar counter where some Coca-cola and soda pop is being served up in the bunches. Jojo pulls out his flask from his inner coat jacket pocket, "You guys need a little spice in your life have a teaspoon of some of the liquid courage whisky to grow some hair on your chest in preparation for the cold winter season." He pours a tablespoon of whisky into glasses of Julio, Conrado, Gerald and his own glass. They raise their glasses in the air "A toast to a good, safe, healthy life boys! Jojo excited to get the party started.

The dance floor is now open, music and dancing has begun. Julio and Joy's eyes meet.

Joy is dancing with someone already. A phonograph record turntable is playing music.

At the ticket booth Filipino Gentlemen are waiting in line in front of the sign that says ".10 Ten Cents A Minute Dance Tickets".

Julio looks at how much money he has brought with him. Five dollars is what he has in five one-dollar bills. He counts his money again, double checks it. He puts four dollars in his pocket.

Julio is the next person in line. The white female dance ticket cashier attendant is working in the booth.

"Next in line please? Hello! How many tickets?" Reassured the Cashier Attendant.

"Ten dance tickets please ma'am!" Shouted Julio!

"That will be one dollar please!" Yelled Cashier Attendant.

Julio takes his ten tickets and puts it in his suit coat jacket pocket. Brushes up and perks up his jacket edges and heads towards the dance floor with a skip in his steps.

At the same time the big band orchestra gets up to the stage, taking their seats and testing out their instruments.

The evening's master of ceremonies a tall slickback brown haired white man gets on the microphone with a deep voice. "Ladies and gentlemen. Boys and girls get your dancing feet ready… The Dance Floor is now open."

At the hall entrance way Big Country Townsman directs a couple of his White Townsmen crew to enter the dance hall while he keeps an eye outside the dance hall building. The White Townsman crewmembers sneak into the place enters behind people into the hall and immediately hides out where no one sees them.

Most white Americans at this time were unsure of who these Filipinos were. Where did they come from? Why are they in America working on the farms? They were called little brown people, Islanders, Boy, Chinks, Monkeys and or Dogs. Most of the Filipinos during this time of American history were hard workers, skilled laborers by day and by night very good dancers, they dressed very well after their day working on the farms, wearing expensive suits, hundred dollar dress shoes, gambled their money frequently, some alcoholics, and they hardly saved up any of that money they earned because they felt what would be the use since going to school was nearly impossible and buying any real estate at this time was also not allowed by the law of the land.

With the jealousy towards the Filipinos building up because there was not many Filipinas around this time Filipino men would be seen around town hanging out with white women even though this was considered illegal at this time. White men would get jealous of the Filipino man because they thought that these Filipino men were taking their woman when in actually these Filipino men were very lonely. The growth of discrimination towards Filipinos during the thirties was widely prevalent and seen by the riots reported in the news of white townsmen rioting and bombing locations of where Filipinos would sleep and hang out at their leisure times.

With the jealousy building up in Big Country Townsman and his white townsmen crew hiding behind the bar counter they see Julio walking around the edges of the dance floor to see what his next moves will be.

"Who is this monkey Julio?" Whispered Big Country Townsman to his three buddies bumping into next to him squatting. "Where did that Julio and his boys

get such nice suits and with what money... they are just farm laborers?"
Whispered one of the Townsman.

Julio and his roommates looking sharp and very handsome step onto the dance
floor. His roomates reach out and grab the hands of their dance partner picks as
Julio makes eye contact with Joy they both offer and share a smile with each
other.

Joy is dancing with another Filipino guy once again a short but stocky looking
Filipino man. So short that he only reaches the shoulders of Joy as she is taller
than he is. The dance floor is starting to fill up. The red light turns on and lights
up the room. A Filipino guy stocky built checks his pockets for more tickets but
he has no more.

Next up is Julio and Joy reaching for each other's hand. He hands her a ticket.

They start to dance. Music sounding from the big band orchestra. Julio
whispers into her ear. "You look wonderful tonight!"

Later that evening Julio is still dancing with Joy. Christian is dancing with
Missy near by him. Julio hands Joy three more dance tickets. With only one left.

"Are you having a fun time?" Comforted Joy.

"Yes I am ma'am having a great time. So good. Here are three tickets in
advance. I will only have one left." Gasphed Julio.

Julio and Joy show their best dance moves.

"Every guy and probably every girl in here has their eyes on you. You look
perfect tonight Joy!" Babbled Julio.

Julio and Joy's dancing has gotten a little slower.

"Only tonight? I see you looking at me every time you come here." Laughed
Joy.

"What do you mean? We look at each other. You're beyond it! You are the most beautiful woman in the world!" Laughed Julio.

"You know every time you come here you only dance me. I think that I would feel much more comfortable if we have more distance from each other." Declared Joy. Both now at arms distance just holding hands dancing. Julio twirls Joy around the room. Julio leading the way with some nice dance moves. The red light turns on with the beam lighting up the room. They continue to dance and enjoy themselves to the music of the Waltz and then into the Foxtrot music played by the orchestra enjoying themselves.

"I don't want you to think that I like you in that way. Remember were only acquaintances and the law cant have us together unless you give me another dance ticket right now please because your additional three minutes is up." Insisted Joy.

The red light turns around. Julio gives another ticket to Joy. They continue to dance.

"Okay great. Joy I have to tell you something I don't believe in courtship ok? It's a waste of time. If I really love the person. I'll tell her right away lovely. But for you I will make an exception ok sweetheart? Just say you love me now Joy, and I will court you forever." Gushed Julio.

Poker faced Joy minding her own dance moves with Julio.

Just as long as Julio knows how she feels about him, would make his evening wonderful. See were not allowed to be with white women unless we paid a dime a dance for it.

The red light turns on and lights up the room signaling dancers to change partners if a current Filipino dance partner had no more dance tickets on hand.

103

"Alright gentlemen if you ain't got no more tickets it was a good night but you got to give another brother a chance to dance." Exclaimed the Master of Ceremonies.

Julio and Joy dance the seconds away as the song changes.

"Do you have anymore tickets? Ticket Please." Sighed Joy. Julio checks his pockets once again with no avail.

"You know it's not ideal we can be together. The law will not allow it outside of this building." Mumbled Joy.

Julio shaking his head and lets go of Joy's hands. Joy smiles at Julio as they part their ways.

"Thank you for the dance. Goodbye." Sighed Julio. Joy is sad faced as another Filipino guy gives her a dance ticket for another minute of dancing.

Afterwards at the rest table seats Julio taps the shoulder of Conrado and the rest of his roommates are taking a load off their feet and no more money to spend for the evening. People watching. The rest of the other dance goers are dancing into the late night.

"Hey I am going back to the bunkhouse." Maintained Julio.

"You going back by yourself?" Laughed Conrado.

"Yeah I will be ok. Got no more money to waste tonight might as well get some shuteye. Better to beat the crowd now than later." Declared Julio.

While the dance party is still going on inside. With no one outside in site. Quite as the wind goes. Julio exits out of the dance hall. "That is strange. It is too quite outside. No one is in eye site."

Simultaneously two White Townsmen are walking to the front of the building.

"Speaking of the devil. I spoke too soon." Julio Whispered. He notices the two townsmen. So he calmly walks towards the side of the building.

The White Townsman notices Julio walking away.

"Hey monkey? Did you eat any dog today?" Yelled one of the two White Townsmen.

Julio picks up the pace, now walking backwards, facing the White Townsmen. The rest of the white townsmen crew are following from behind, trying to catch up, many yards away.

"Oh yea and you are a white monkey. I'm not a monkey I'm Filipino!" Stammered Julio. Julio runs and sprints down the long side of the dance hall building. The two townsmen try to chase Julio down but they can't keep up and they decided to stop running after him. Breathing hard. Catching their breath.

"Come back here! You need a Job? Go on then go eat your dogs!" Cautioned White Townsmen. The rest of the Townsmen crew as well as Big Country Townsmen shows up behind them. "What you out here yelling for boy?"

"One of them Filipino monkeys just ran away!" Cried White Townsmen.

"Or do you mean? You were just too slow to catch him son. Well just wait for the rest of them as they come out of the Manila dance hall." Laughed Big Country Townsman.

At the same time this is going on Julio runs as fast as he can on the dirt roads till he

can't hardly catch his breath again, he stops and takes a rest for a moments sake. "I think I lost them. Thank you Lord."

"Alright" Julio tries to run and pick up the pace. Julio jogs for some time and falls to his knees. He takes a seat by one of the big trees on the road of large trees, he places his head on the trunk of the tree catching his breath and now is at peace. No signs of the White Townsmen in clear site.

"It feels uncomfortable at this moment. All alone in my new home this so called free country." Murmured Julio closing his eyes. The sounds of the wind from the fields. His eye quickly opens and closes, staying low to the ground trying not to be seen. Remaining calm and relaxed.

"Lord if you can only hear me now." Whispered Julio to himself.

Layback looking into the night's stars. "I feel lost in life is there any hope God? Help me Lord. Angel of healing heal my wounds, my pains so you can make me an instrument of your peace."

Nothing but the night's skylights up Julio's natural surroundings. A shooting star comes across the night's sky. He closes his eye makes a silent wish. Julio enjoying his time all-alone.

"Beautiful, thank you for this life of mine. There is enough light that I think I can do some writing." Julio takes out his paper and pen out of his pocket jacket "What will I write about? I think I will write a nice poem called *For My Joy Dance Step Moves.*" He begins to write on his paper while whispering back to himself to get it right.

Roses are red,
Violets are blue,
Your dancing is joy,
And so are you.

Orchids are white,

106

Ghost ones are rare,

Marbles are shiny,

And so is your hair.

Magnolia grows,

With buds like eggs,

Cells are smooth,

And so are your legs.

Sunflowers reach,

Up to the skies,

Jeans are blue,

And so are your eyes.

Foxgloves in hedges,

Surround the farms,

Parts are soft,

And so are your arms.

Daisies are pretty,

Daffies have style,

Your manner is friendly,

And so is your smile.

A dance step move is beautiful,

Just like you.

His eyes begin to slowly close as he begins falling asleep into a dreaming state while holding his paper and pen laying on his chest.

In his dream Julio wakes up to an open green land in a sweat early in the morning, running through the tall corn fields, enjoying his time attending to the Philippine Islands farm fields, plowing one of the areas with his *Carabao* better known as a water buffalo that is native to the Philippines.

"Good job King Carabao let's go!" Yelled Julio. The Carabao takes off forward at an unexpected delayed rate of time that the force surprises Julio as he is accidentally thrown off of it backwards and falling onto the muddy ground.

He gets up standing on two feet feeling his arms and legs to see if any broken bones, "Am I alive? Am I ok?" Julio said screaming shocked but grateful he is perfectly fine picks himself off whipping off the mud covering his eyes.

Julio working in another part of the farm decides it is time to now do the harvesting of the green stock crops of the yellow white corn that are now thirteen feet tall using his bolo knife amongst the tall pineapple trees and coconut trees as his blue skyline backdrop from a far as the eye can see. At the chicken feeding area he is now feeding the chickens. Picking up eggs that are newly laid against the hay.

Meanwhile at the present day news press conference with Christian and the news crews he is passionately sharing one of his stories during his early life experiences on the farm fields of the Philippines before coming to America, "In those days when we lived in the Philippines we actually felt free with no worries at all but the opportunity in this land of the so called free sounded to good of an opportunity for us not to pass up!"

With the remaining corn from his days harvest Julio is using it as feeding food for the chickens making sure they get their feed for the day. Whistling while he works humming hymns of his joyfulness. At the same time he starts picking up eggs that were laid by them making sure to gather all that were left by the chickens.

"America brought my Filipino brothers and I to a big land where freedom comes with a price & sacrifice. Feels like it is illegal to be a Filipino in America during that time of the nineteen thirties era" says Christian telling the news crews his story describing what he saw and felt while working on the farm lands.

A noise from the nearby bushes a couple of yards away rattles the nerves waking up Julio all of a sudden from his deep dream state that was taking place as he tries to continue to take shelter cover and rest from the night. Nothing but the sound of the wind blows through the sky. "Hoy! Who goes der?" said Julio who is startled breathing deeply. All that can be seen in the night are the whites in his eyes and the shine from the moon and stars above guiding the nights view of the ever changing scenery for him to imagine the reality that he is currently in.

"Wow the moon is so bright it lights up the area around me, I got this song in my head I need to get it out of my head and write it down the light looks just a bit perfect right about now I think I will take out my paper and pen hidden in my jacket and start to do some writing" says Julio at the same time taking out his paper and pen from his inside suit jacket.

"Ok here is the song it goes a little something like this I call this song, *The Tale of My Maganda Dime A Dance Girl Crush.*"

109

It began on a lonely Friday, Summer evening:

I was the hardest working farmworker around,

She was the most maganda dime a dance girl in town.

She was my crush,

My maganda crush,

My dime a dance girl.

We used to dance so well together,

Back then.

We wanted to run together, around the world,

We wanted it all.

But one evening, one lonely evening,

We decided to run too much.

Together we hit a White Townsman.

It was long, so long of a night

From that moment our relationship changed.

She grew so hard to love.

And then it happened:

Oh no! Oh no!

She thrown a rock at the White Townsmen Crew.

Alas, a White Townsmen Crew!

My crush thrown a rock at the White Townsmen Crew.
It was quick, so quick.

The next day I thought my lips had broken,
I thought my dancing feet had burst into flames,
(But I was actually overreacting a little.)

But still, she is in my thoughts night and day.
I think about how it all changed that evening,
That lonely Friday, Summer evening dance.

My chest... ouch!
When I think of that maganda dime a dance girl,
That maganda dime a dance girl is a joy to me .
My crush!"

"What a song great someday I will sing that to Joy well maybe." Says Julio as he then stops writing, folds up him papers and then places back his pen and paper into his jacket pocket as the full moon shines from above with the calm of the night and humid breeze in the air he looks up into the sky that he cannot help but to shut his eyes Julio now completely falls asleep he begins to snore loud into the night matching the same tempo as the wind blowing in the air that night.

4

Manila Dance Hall the Filipino Farmer's life

In the morning the Filipino farm workers are working hard on the farm fields turning the soil with their tools and some with their bare hands with signs of blood underneath their fingernails building up tending to care for mother natures lands. Wearing handkerchiefs covering their noses, mouths and sombrero hat to take cover from the yellow orange sun shining upon the Filipinos.

Coming towards their way is Mr. Kenny Good the farm's manager with his receding hairline comb over drives up whistling to his own musical tunes gets out of his truck puts his straw hat on with a full set of roosters crowing in its cages on the back pickup truck cargo bed. Mr. Good gets the attention waving down, yelling towards and calling his workers. "All right great job men take a break gentlemen. It is picnic time!"

The Filipino farm workers repeating together in unison shouting, "Picnic Time!" Cheers and applause erupt from the workers. A few of the Filipino farm workers find some energy and start whistling sounds while assisting taking out the cages of roosters, lifting them off the truck bed one by one carefully. More Filipino farm workers get ready as they choose their best fighting rooster from the given row of cages based on the loudest crowing one.

The rest of the onlookers in the crowd use their hard earned money start to count it for a possible wager gambling bet. Christian follows through by being also inconspicuous in counting his money in public. Conrado looking at him. "You going to bet all your money Christian?"

"That game cock rooster sure looks and sounds like a winner. Look doesn't it look strong and confident?" Exclaimed Christian pointing at the rooster.

The landlords associate gambling bookie managers are walking around taking bets and passes by Christian who is signaling to him to make a bet. Christian hands him all his money in his pocket. The cock fight begins with cheers from the crowd. The gamecocks fight for quite some time till one of the other roosters doesn't move all of a sudden maybe from last jumping in the air move they collide and it went straight down. Referee presents the winner to the roar of the crowd.

After a long day the Filipino farm workers break bread buy serving up a feast. Eating Chicken. Finishing up eating what is left. Half of the roommates are still eating while the others are changing their clothes and preparing for the evenings outings.

"*Masarap! Unay naumbag nasayaat!* Very good! We have to get freshened up now and get ready for tonight boys!" Yelled Julio. He takes a break takes out his writing journal, a pen and starts to do some writing, "Let me write real quick a poem called *The Dance Instructor and the Dime A Dance Woman.*"

See the dancing of the Filipino man,
I think he's angry at the American plan.

He finds it hard to see the dance ticket,
Overshadowed by the big tree townsmen.

Who is that gambling near the gambling tables
I think she'd like to eat with that money.

She is but a good broad woman,
Admired as she sits upon more Filipinos wanting to score a dance.

Her fresh dress is just a repeat from the last,
like the other dime a dance woman.
It needs no wash yet, because the next is the same as the rest.

She's not alone she brings a dress,
a pet cat, and lots of water to digest.

The cat likes to chase a Filipino in a suit,
Especially one that's in the fruit farm fields all day money in the pockets dance
the night away.

The man shudders at buying a new ticket
He want to leave but this woman wants the money for a tip or another dime a
dance.

   That night at the Manila dance hall Julio and his Filipino roommates are
drinking soda pop cola at the eating social table. Card games are also being
played by a few others of the bunk house mates at the corners of the room but

with no monetary bets just for the thrills of seeing what kind of hands they can be dealt with the flip of the wrist of the cards just before their big almond eyes of honesty and good morals yes it is a good day in the neighborhood of Watsonville California Philippine USA.

At the same time at the doorway of the dance hall Big Country Townsman and the White Townsmen are making their way in line to get into the hall but they are stopped at end of the long line to get in by other paying Filipinos but Big Country towering over everyone sees through the doorway that Julio is at the table in plain sites view.

"Lets see what these monkeys are up to boys." Snapped Big Country Townsman. Filipinos in front of the White Townsmen crew is let in ahead of them. The bouncer stops and holds the line with the White Townsmen next to enter the dance hall.

"I'm sorry boys we are filled to capacity tonight. No one is allowed in anymore for the night." Declared Security Bouncer.

Big Country Townsman leaves then comes back looks and peeks through the side window of the dance hall. He sees Julio dancing with Joy.

Meanwhile inside the Manila Dance Hall with a full dance floor moving their feet to the rhythm of the big band orchestra. The last dance sign is displayed and paraded by the dance patron attendant on the stage, as the round clock on the wall is about to reach two in the morning. The red light beams across the room.

As Julio makes his way towards the front entrance of the dance hall he is just about to step out of the building he hears some men outside talking he slowly peeks outside and notices the White Townsmen crew gathering outside the front of the dance hall.

"Anytime now them Filipino monkeys will be coming out. Patience men." Declared Big Country Townsman.

Julio rushes back to alert his roommates. Walking backwards back into the dance hall Julio stumbles, trips, crawling and getting back up.

"Spsss. Hoy" Whispered Julio. As he is trying to be quiet, tip toeing towards his bunkhouse mates. "They are out front let's leave take the back exit real quick avoid any violence that may arise again."

Julio and his roommates Jojo, Conrado, Gerald, Binong, Christian, Boy Isagani and Soriano quietly make a dash and escape out of towards the back exit of the dance hall.

At the same time another of the White Townsman notices Julio running away out from the back of the dance hall with his housemates following one after the other is Jojo, Conrado, Gerald, Binong, Christian, Boy Isagani, and Soriano.

"Hey there go those monkeys! They are over here boys!" Yelled another White Townsman. He waves down his crew whistles them to go towards chasing them now.

As the white townsmen crew who has their own sticks and three fire torches chasing after the Filipinos who are well ahead already by at least one hundred yards away into the darkness of the land as the moon shines bright into the night. Big Country Townsman is the slowest and last of the bunch.

"Go get them boys! Hurry! Chase after them monkeys!" Commanded Big Country Townsman.

The Filipino housemates split up into pairs going in different directions and disappearing Into the fields. The White townsmen running out of breath stop together when they reach the end of the field with no visibility of the Filipinos anymore.

Back at the Manila dance hall back yard door looking out towards the backyard chase of the Filipinos by the White Townsmen crew is the dime a dance woman Joy, Missy and her other girlfriends.

"Them Filipino men sure are quick they are really something special girls right?" Exclaimed Joy.

"Oh yes they are really cute, dress well, handsome, they can dance and they got money. They would be great husbands." Laughed Missy.

Meanwhile out in the open field running as fast as they can. No site of the White Townsmen can be seen anymore. Julio, Conrado, Soriano, Jojo, Gerald, Binong, Christian and Boy Isagani, take a rest real quick and catch their breath.

"I think we lost them gentlemen," gasped Julio.

Out of all the guys the last one to catch up is Boy Isagani breathing louder than any of the guys. "Ahhhh. I can hardly breathe oh my God. Oh my God. Help me lord."

As they approached the cross section of the road all of the Filipino housemates are composing themselves from the non-stop sprinting. Catching their breath with a quick break from the action. Huffing and puffing they normally do not run this fast.

"Man why is it we are always on the run. We never did any crime." Maintained Conrado.

Julio pointing at each guy around him. "Well hell yeah that crime is that we, that's you, you, you, all of you pares are Filipino. Puro Pinoy! We can not ever talk our language here in America if we want jobs."

117

All the guys' hands are on their knees, hands behind their heads bodies upright exhausted.

Julio takes a nearby seat on the ground with his fellow housemates following his lead.

A noise is coming out from a distance heard by Christian. What's that noise? Sounds like a vehicle."

Coming down the dirt road split between two farm fields Julio along with his Filipino housemates Conrado, Soriano, Jojo, Gerald, Binong, Christian and Boy Isagani notice a car coming towards them from afar. The gentlemen lie down and try to hide themselves on the side
of the road laying flat on their face. The car passes them by. They lift their heads and turns to it towards the direction the car went in unison. They get up and pat themselves down from the dirt road dust.

"Boys that was a close one." Gasphed Jojo.

"You can say that again." Blurted Christian.

"Yes so close our nice suits are dirty again." Cried Conrado.

"You guys just be happy you have nice clothes." Says Boy Isagani.

At the same time an associate white townsman driver is with Big Country Townsman cruising the area scooping it out in their 1930 Ford Model A Touring Sedan car.

"You think we will find those dog monkeys boss?" Admired White Townsman Driver

"You mean Filipinos Joe? They're out here somewhere son. Someone has to attend to the fields around here. Thats some hard work manual skilled labor from the finest islands on God's green gracious earth." Commanded Big Country Townsman.

The sedan moves onwards on the road as the moon shines bright.

On the ground the Filipino gentlemen get up off the ground, dust themselves off and run off.

"Gentlemen let's get out of here fast *napardas!*" Commanded Julio.

Later at night back safely at the Filipino housing barracks most of the Filipino farm worker housemates are sound asleep except for Julio. Julio is reading a letter mailed from the Philippines. The letter hand written and signed by his Ex-girlfriend.

The letter reads, "I have gone and married already here in the Philippines. I kindly wish that you forget about me and go on with your life and do things that make you happy to have a better life for yourself, Love Mary Jane Villanueva Napenas."

"I can not believe this is happening." Maintained Julio. Julio crumbles the letter and throws it onto the floor. The noise wakes up Jojo. Jojo picks up the crumbled letter on the floor and throws it at Julio, which falls to the ground.

"Man pare keep our place clean! Go to sleep! Keep dreaming but go to sleep we got a lot of work to do early in the morning by sunrise on the fields." Whispered Jojo.

Julio picks up the crumpled letter, steps outside, throws the letter out toward the darkness, and takes a seat on the steps.

"I came to America for a better life a better future. It is hard to survive and save money here. What am I living for? Why do I feel like a criminal here in America? While I am on this land, I'm going to be the best dancer and teacher.

I'm going to make some changes and make myself happy. Love myself. I will be a legend. Make History. Become A Pensionado!" talking to himself demanded Julio. He decides to pick up his banjo guitar strumming it grabs his writing papers and grabs his pen back by his bedside then taking a seat on the front porch steps of the bunk house he begins to write venting out his frustrations on the recent news he decides to write, "I will call this song *Like A Wooden Banjo.*"

I heard there was a secret banjo
That Mary Jane Villanueva *Napenas knew about, and it pleased the dance hall*
manager
But you don't really care for drums, do ya?
Well, it goes like this
The fourth, the fifth
The minor fall and the major lift
The baffled dance hall manager yells Last Dance Done

Done move on love yourself
Done move on love yourself
Done move on love yourself
Done move on love yourself

I'm not here to say I'm a wooden puppy
I'm not here to lie to you

Some people wait a lifetime

For a banjo like this

Some people search forever

For that one wooden banjo

Ohh I can't believe it's happening to me

Some people wait a lifetime

For a banjo like this to make a song

I'm not here to say I'm a wooden puppy

I'm not here to lie to you

There's still a little bit of your heart on my mind

There's still a little bit of you laced with my doubt

It's still a little hard to say what's going on

There's still a little bit of your hand, your smooth hand holding mine

There's still a little bit of your lips I haven't danced in a while

You step a little closer each day that I can't say what's going on

A ticket taught me to dance more

Love taught me to drink and dance

Life taught me to run a farm

So it's not hard to fall

When you dance like a good heart

The baffled dance hall manager yells Last Dance Done

Done move on love yourself

Done move on love yourself

Done move on love yourself

Done move on love yourself

And if we're only here once I wanna dance with you

You've got something I need

In this world full of drums there's one loving me

And if we're only here once (done)

I wanna dance with you (you, you, you)

You've got something I need

In this world full of drums there's one loving me

And if we're only here once (done)

I wanna dance with you (you, you)

Skies are wooden, I am happy

Catching drums in my hands

Only silence as it's ending

Like we never had a chance

Do you have to make me feel happy?

You can take the smooth ticket

You can break my feet

Like I'm made of drums

Like I'm made of drums

Go on and try to tear me down

I will be rising from the ground

Like a smooth ticket

Like a loud shoe

Who knows what miracles

You can achieve

When you dance dance dance

Somehow you will

You will when you dance

I'm not here to say I'm a wooden puppy

I'm not here to lie to you

I'm here to dance with you again maybe one last time

I've finally thought it through

I'm not here to drink

I'm not giving up (done)

I'm here to dance

To dance is my goal

The baffled dance hall manager yells Last Dance Done move on love yourself.

Julio looks up into the starlit night sky and smiles in victory for another good writing session, he looks at the writings he has written on the paper and takes a deep breath in relief.

"I got a another I will call this song *Farm Song.*"

My fertile farmland, you inspire me to write, write, write.
I love the way you sprouts, water and grows,
Invading my mind during the day and dancing through the night,
Always dreaming about the lively life of mine too the max.

Let me compare you to a great boat ship
You are more hostile, nutritious and nice.
Plump sun heats the antic peaches of June,
And summertime has the gigantic corn.

How do I love you? Let me count the ways.
I love your rich harvest, seeds and farming.
Thinking of your frantic seeds fills my days.
My love for you is the big prince charming.

Now I must away with a manic heart,
Remember my right words whilst we're apart
While I dance dance all night.

Julio takes a deep breath in relief as he gets up from the steps, looks out towards the star skies and sees a falling star. Closes his eyes. Makes a wish walks inside and falls asleep for the night.

The next day on the farm a line is forming with the white farm-recruiting managers checking the hands of the newly arrived Filipinos coming off of a truck. A Filipino and Mexican day laborers approach the white farm recruiter.

"Ok you are hired, next show the palm of your hands please." Exclaimed White Farm Recruiter.

Next a Mexican day laborer shows out his hands.

"Ahh. Why are your hands so clean and so fresh so clean? Sorry no work." Insisted White Farm Recruiter. White recruiter gestures for the Mexican day laborer to take a step aside.

Craig Leonardo Santos a new Filipino farm worker recruit takes a step up and shows his hands, which are pretty rough looking, callused, tough, thick and strong.

"Ok you speak English?" Spat White Recruiter.

"Okay! Yes Sir! I speak little English but good with my hands Sir!" Laughed Craig Leonardo Santos the new Filipino farm recruit. "Ok then", said white farm recruiter gestures and points to the direction to go behind him.

Later that morning the Filipino farm workers who are working the fields, a group of the Filipinos wave at welcoming in open arms Craig Leonardo Santos the new Filipino making his way to start his first day of farming work in America.

"Welcome pare!" Comforted Julio. Craig the new Filipino goes down the row of Filipino farm workers. Greeting and paying respects to his new band of brothers he finds an open space learning, training and duplicating along side the Filipino next to him working the fields.

Julio and the rest of his co-farm workers attend to the fields as they see another new Pinoy a five foot five black hair brown eyed strong looking lean and chiseled Patrick Cruz Serrano who gets recruited from a distance ahead of them giving him the thumbs up after inspecting the palms of his hands.

"There goes another one of us" Laughed Julio.

"Yeah that's good! They are getting work, most of the new ones don't have the right looking rough hands." Reassured Conrado.

Patrick the new Pinoy watches the other Filipino workers attending to the fields and copies to what they are doing. Like an assembly line system Julio breaks out his dance moves as the rest of the gentlemen enjoy their work and take a break and they start to dance strut their best dance moves down the dirt row gravel line.

Jojo picks up the banjo guitar he has laid out by the side of the road and starts to play his guitar. "Go on now boys! Ok show your best dance move now!" The Filipino farm workers dancing down the line and stretching out their bodies on the side while they wait their turn to strut their best dance moves down the line shaking off the tension from all the bent over hard work.

"Oh I have a new great song I wrote to go with this melody boys" Julio speaking above the noise levels of the banjo guitar. "Sing it Julio! Sing it!" Jojo shouts out loud towards Julio. "Alright this song is called *How much do I love singing and dancing?*" says Julio as the Filipino gentlemen dance along to the musical tunes down the dance line.

126

I get on with life as a skilled farm laborer,

I'm a handsome dancing kinda person.

I like dancing on Sundays,

I like boxing in the week.

I like to contemplate dancing.

But when I start to daydream,

My mind turns straight to singing.

Five six seven eight...

Sometimes I look at myself and I look into my eyes,

I notice the way I think about singing with a smile,

Bolo on my side ready to make the soil fine.

But I think it's dancing making my life worthwhile.

Why is it so hard for me to decide which I love more?

Dancing or...

Singing?

I like to use words like 'hoy,'

I like to use words like 'pare.'

I like to use words about dancing.

But when I stop my talking,

My mind turns straight to singing.

Five six seven eight...

Sometimes I look at myself and I look into my eyes,
I notice the way I think about singing with a smile,
Bolo on my side ready to make the soil fine.
But I think it's dancing making my life worthwhile.
Why is it so hard for me to decide which I love more?
Dancing or...
Singing?

   I like to hang out with Jojo,
   I like to kick back with Christian,
   But when left alone,
   My mind turns straight to singing.

      Five six seven eight...

Sometimes I look at myself and I look into my eyes,
I notice the way I think about singing with a smile,
Bolo on my side ready to make the soil fine.
But I think it's dancing making my life worthwhile.
Why is it so hard for me to decide which I love more?
Dancing or...
Singing?

   I'm not too fond of bullies,

I really hate fighting,
But I just think back to singing,
And I'm happy once again.

Five six seven eight.

"Yay very good very good pare!" Soriano yelling from the other end of the dance line. "Shhh quiet down" whispered and waving everyone down to cut the talking Jojo and the banjo guitar that he strumming away with make their way down the dance line now it is Julio's turn to dance down the line. Showing his best dance moves he begins to dance down the line he notices the farm manager's eyes makes eye contact with his, "Uh oh guys back to work now!" Mr. Good the white farm manager catches them notices them playing around playing music and dancing on the field like a freestyle swing dance line.

"Hey I see you guys! Hey you monkeys! Stop playing and dancing around and get back to work please!" Commanded Mr. Good as he was trotting along the dirty road towards the Filipinos.

The Filipino farm workers laugh, and continue to quarrel pushing each other playfully with the guys getting back to attending to their field work with dirt and blood underneath their nails from all the farm work to be done. The farm manager with his hands on his waste pointing at the Filipino farm workers.

"Back to work! Thank you." Demanded Mr. Good. He takes a walk towards his car and then towards the farm's shack across the road out of the Filipinos sight.

"Work work work. Let's get back to work gentlemen." Laughed Julio shuffling the dirt soil right below him.

"That's all we ever do is work. It is like we have no choice. I thought we were supposed to be free when we came here." Sighed Christian

As the Filipino farm workers work the fields. Christian finds some few rocks. "What are these?" As Christian picks up some of the pebble sized rocks and places them into his pockets.

"Christian what are those? Your afternoon snack?" Gushed Julio.

The Filipino Farm workers continue work on farm fields getting all sweaty and dirty. Baking in the warm sun.

Afterwards in the day Mr. Good the farm's manager walks up to the field of Filipino farm

workers with a sack of cash. "Alright boys it is payday gather around in a single file line. Ok here you go. Good job. One dollar for you. Ok one for you. Keep up the good work boy. One dollar for you. Ok now." Mr. Good the Farm Manager gives one dollar to each farm worker.

Julio approaches the Mr. Good and receives his one-dollar in his hands "Thank you Sir Good God Bless you" Mr. Good smiles and Julio walks off and waits to the side to wait for his bunkhouse mates in the long line already formed with over one hundred Filipinos waiting to get paid Julio decides to take out his pen and paper and write a song while taking a break, "I think I will title this new song lyrics, *Always Stay Loyal, Mr. Good.*"

I grew up overshadowed by a flat valley
Couldn't catch the eye of no city boy

Here I am devoted to Mr. Good

How I love the way you look in your blue jeans

Can't believe I let the smog cloud my eye

Where the flat valley stands

And the green mountains surround our lands

I'll ride my power truck with you by my side just as long as you keeping paying

us

There's a whisper in the California Central Valley breeze

Reminding me of dancing with white broads

That whisper builds

That whisper cries

Dancing in the morning skies

You appear on the horizon

Brushing that curly hair from your eyes

The city folk with their fancy clothing and cars

Cement valley like grey tombs

Don't have nothin' on our way of life

Just listen to the stream river

Don't live your life like a poor

131

Today might feel a time to be like a poor
But that ain't no way to lead a good life

You know, there's a lot I drive by in my power truck
Folk who is messing up
Always stay loyalty, Mr. Good
Always stay loyalty

In California Central Valley, when I was a child
I met a loyalty man
"How can you be so loyalty?" asked I
Here was his wise reply

Don't live your life like a poor
Today might feel a time to be like a poor
But that ain't no way to lead a good life

Met an old lady who lived like a poor
"What happened to her?" asked I
Here was his wise reprise

Don't live your life like a poor
Today might feel a time to be like a poor
But that ain't no way to lead a good life

That lady's gone now
It's sad really
Word is, she had curly hair once

Little Mr. Good, keep your jeans blue
Always stay loyalty, Mr. Good
Always stay loyalty

Stream river, stream river, stream river
Stream river, stream river, stream river.

Other Filipino farm workers who got their dollar for their days work are gathered around Julio listening to him as he puts his paper and pen away into his jacket pocket. Next up to get his dollar is the a new Filipino recruit, "Really? All this hard work and we get $1 dollar?"

"Boy you've only been here for four hours today. It is too darn hot out here to be arguing with you." Groaned Mr. Good.

The New Filipino walks off with his one dollar looking like he is calculating the math in his head.

"Four quarters times four equals one dollar! Got it!" Exclaimed New Filipino. Mr. Good looks down the line and there is a long line building up.

"There's more of ya'll. Form another line next to here please. There you go. Quickly sign here. Thank you. Come on step it up get your money." Shouted Mr. Good.

Two lines are being formed now the line gets shorter. A couple of skilled Filipino farmers wave themselves with their dollar to cool themselves down from the heat.

Later that day the Filipino farm workers are all gathered around their various recreational groups. One group is doing boxing drills and another group is doing eskrima kali stick fighting drills and exercises.

Another Filipino group is practicing their ballroom dance skills with Julio as the main dance instructor.

"One two, one two, there you go!" Exclaimed Julio.

The third group is playing card games and gambling. A fourth group of Filipinos with Conrado are playing some basketball on a wooden backboard and peach basket elevated to

ten feet attached to a tall tree trunk.

"You got this! Yes! Nice shot!" Shouted Conrado.

A fifth group with Christian is practicing their boxing skills with punching mitts and gloves while making the sounds "Pop pop, pop pop. Yeah. Good punch." Says Christian. Another group is also shadow boxing.

A few of the Filipino farm works make their way inside the bunk house only two Filipino guys left are reading and writing in the corner of the house porch of the farm camp bunk house with the sun setting from the distance one of them that is writing is Julio. "Oh buddy I just wrote a new song who wants to hear it? Oh well here it goes I titled it *Relaxing in a Peaceful Quiet Place"*

Fun time playing and learning
You can take it or leave it

Blue sunny cool skies nice time to reach into the recreation box
I walk through her hills and walk on her white sand clear blue waters

Relaxing peaceful quiet place
Together we cry
Seeing nature down the california coast was the most fun candy to the eye ,
oh my thank you Lord.
God shed his grace on thee

Just us young Pinoy Ilocano boys with the shiny dance shoes and fancy sharp suits and ties
God shed his grace on thee
Boats cars and train vehicles so far the best inventions the good Lord bestowed among
monongs.
Cause she's my companion all along the coast

Relaxing peaceful quiet place
Together we cry
Seeing nature down the california coast was the most fun candy to the eye oh my
thank you Lord God shed his grace on thee relaxing peaceful quiet abundant natural lands"

Julio claps his hands and raises them high into the air in victory for finishing writing and singing that song and then he takes his steps to start off the dancing with the Filipinos that he sees starting to dance and cheers them on from afar while quickly approaching them. "It's time to get ready for tonight gentlemen. Get your suits and dancing shoes on."

Afterwards back at the farm housing camp the Filipino brothers begin to get ready for the nights festivities. Shining their shoes, shaving, getting dressed, fixing their ties, listening to the radio music, practicing their dance moves, fixing their hair in the mirror.

At the same time at the Manila dance mall the dime a dance white women are getting themselves all dolled up and ready for the night of dancing. The women are bonding between each other and laughing at nonsense as they put on their makeup and dresses for the night. Joy and her best friend Missy check themselves on last minute touch ups in front of the mirror.

"Hey Missy, so you ready for tonight's dancing?" Babbled Joy.

"Joy, I should be asking you that question girlfriend." Laughed Missy.

"Me?" Soothed Joy.

"Yes! Shouted Missy.

"Well I hope Julio the best dancer in town will be there he's like a Filipino Fred Astaire or Filipino Bing Crosby and guess what? He gave me a paper with a song that he wrote the night before, do you girls want to hear it?" All the girls in the room who heard Joy say this all turn towards Joy. "Yes girl friend sing it girl!" her best friend Missy declares out loud. Joy stands up and recites "the name of the song is titled, *In the Ticket Booth Closet Full of Coat Jackets and Top Hats We Dance*"

Walking the beaches of the blue lagoon Pagudpud
Let your waves crash down on me head against my chest
Working the farms by day dancing the beauties by night alright
We were both and it felt so right we dance

In the closet full of coat jackets and hats
Time to buy and time to lose
Learning and practicing how to write right dance consistently
The sea is high while kissing you the beauty right

Games songs dances
We were striking matches just to watch 'em burn
Sun and blue skies both our feet walk the white sand blue shores
Misty water-colored memories

In the closet full of coat jackets and hats we dance
Time to buy and time to lose
Learning and practicing how to write right dance consistently
The sea is high while kissing we dance

"What a song girl! You must be the beauty! Girl how do you know he is like Fred Astaire and Bing Crosby?" Laughed Missy.

"The way he moves. The energy he brings. How he holds me in his arms and lifts me into the sky oh my girl! You've seen him dancing and singing in the movies. Well he dances like him maybe even better. Plus he wrote more songs on this piece of paper girls you can't even imagine the magic he wrote on this look! You've seen him dance with me until he has no more tickets" Admired Joy. She gets up and shows the girls a little two step they all laugh and cheer her on.

5

Filipino American Farms, Sing and Dance

Meanwhile the Filipino gentlemen are back in their farm camp room between them are split up with one group drinking and rehearsing their dance moves with Julio, Conrado, Boy, Christian and another Filipino farm workers from a nearby agricultural laborers housing camp. While the remaining men Jojo, Gerald, Binong, and Soriano are drinking and playing card games.

"Hoy, come on guys we got to get your swing dance moves smoother and more graceful as I take a break and write this song about you dancing love birds." Reassured Julio. He takes out his paper and pen out of his jacket and begins to think for a moment and then begins to proceed to write, "Let us name this song called, *This Pain"*

We can let it burn until it bled choose

Think that I could have been so scared so disconnected

From the lies they talk to the surface

Things that we love and give her courage

On you and me there's saturn

You don't wanna stop you're breathing on the day

Call it won't be the same call me gay

Sorry I'm so afraid

Alcohol burns warm with every kiss my heart this pain

End so I danced it for I that this maybe our last dance

Wits you've got a single silver bullet tonight we'll celebrate

The end look into your life so this is why we dance not to feel this pain

Us down now you're gone well, I was just thinking

About you, but I had dance moves too slow and I hope

I find someone who feels the touch of your skin

Run the frames through next week's edition

Alcohol burns warm with every kiss my heart this pain

End so I jumped it

Wits you've got a single silver bullet tonight we'll celebrate

The end look into your life so this is why we dance not to feel this pain

Screen screaming for help for your silence means
Marvelous episodes of pain blistered hands
Pore and you wonder what it's all the empty dancing shoes
Under the moon at all stone by stone throw

Alcohol burns warm with every kiss my heart this pain
End so I danced it.
Wits you've got a single silver bullet tonight we'll celebrate.
The end look into your life so this is why we dance not to feel this pain

Some of the guys still dancing in the foreground of where Julio is singing what he wrote are clumsy but quickly getting a hang of the dance steps. Julio gets back to writing his next song talking to himself with his bunk mates looking at him, "Alright I got poem on my mind I will call this poem *Filipino Ballroom.*"

All that is little is not a venue,
venue, by all account is large.
Does the venue make you shiver?
does it? Make you move.

An ancient amphitheater, however hard it tries,
Will always be massive.
Anatomical, ancient amphitheater.
Does the ancient amphitheater make you shiver?
does it? Make you move.

The zany, filled foyer sings like a marble
Like Water.
Why is it so zany?

A dark dining room, however hard it tries,
    Will always be big.
Are you upset by how generous it is?
    Does it tear you apart to see the dark dining room so intense?

I saw the the stunning room of my generation destroyed,
    How I mourned the adjacent anteroom.
Now surprising is just the thing,
    To get me wondering if the adjacent anteroom is impressive.

I saw the stuffy people of my generation destroyed,
    How I mourned the gambling and drinking room.
Now unventilated is just the thing,
    To get me wondering if the room is airless.
It is much better dancing in our barracks but no kababaihan woman
    for you to get to know ok lang.

Julio smiling of nodding in agreement in what he sees from the group of
Filipino dancers getting their dance moves down much better. Each of the
Filipino bunk mates who are dancing partner up and act as each dance partner

with one of them leading the dance. Looking smooth and graceful with each step at a time.

All bets are in at the table Jojo, Gerald, Binong and Soriano as the games dealer. One after the other starting with Jojo begin to hold their cards tight and close to their face covering their mouths slowly checking back and forth at their card in hands.

"Alright boys since I'm this games dealer it is time to show your cards." Whispered Soriano.

Jojo shows his cards he has a five and ten. Gerald shows his cards he has queen of diamonds and ten. Binong shows his cards he has a joker spades and a seven. Soriano shows his cards and he has an Ace diamonds and King Diamonds.

"Excuse me boys but got a blackjack winner!" Shouted Soriano. Soriano takes in all the money in the middle of the table and starts stacking his money. Cleaning the money from

Jojo, Gerald and Binong all but have left is one coin each in their hands.

Christian, Boy, Julio are leading the dance lessons on one side of the room while Jojo, Conrado who runs up to an open chair, Gerald and a couple of other Filipino farm workers are playing their card games to pass by the time.

"Ok gentlemen. Watch here first. Back straight. Ok one two, one two, and one two. That fair enough? Ok your turn." Insisted Julio.

During these days, the time we had off to pass the time was filled with recreational activities as well as gambling and dancing.

At the dining table Conrado places his bet. Binong, Soriano and Jojo watch what he is doing at the moment.

"Are you sure you want to place that high of a wager? You don't want to lose all of your days pay!" Reassured Jojo as he run's real quick to follow the dance routines going on the other side of the room.

"Don't worry pare! I got me a good hand. Plus I heard since winter is approaching their maybe some job openings up north in Alaska or Seattle at the fish canneries looking for people good with their hands." Consoled Conrado.

"Really? Could use some new work for the new season." Comforted Gerald.

Jojo comes back to the table to see the next card hand moves in action. From a distance dance practice is continuing with Julio as the lead with Christian and several more additional

Filipinos from the other camps. The Filipino gentlemen Conrado, Jojo, Binong, Soriano, and Gerald are still playing card games.

Wen!! Pare! You should check out these job opportunities if you like! Or be a D.I. Like Julio! You know Dance Instructor. Alright, what do you guys have?" Shouted Conrado as final bets are made and Conrado gets a full house and wins the pot of money.

"Congratulations Conrado you can now dance with any woman for as long as your money will last." Exclaimed Jojo.

In the corner of the room of the bunkhouse practicing their dance moves one step at a time. Julio is leading his Filipino brothers with dancing steps "Yes gentlemen that is it one two, one two nice and easy men."

The groups of Filipinos take a two steps distance between each other spreading out in line formation arm lengths apart with Julio taking the lead. The remaining Filipino gentlemen who were playing cards Jojo, Conrado, Jojo, Binong, Soriano, and Gerald join in the dance rehearsal.

"Hey there's enough of us here we can partner up. One will be the male lead the other the female dancer." Declared Christian.

All the guys in the room partner up and practice their dance moves. While this is going on Julio makes his way to stand on top of something overlooking the vast group of Filipinos.

"Alright brothers let's get ready for tonight!" Exclaimed Julio.

All the Filipinos in the room scrambling and quickly moving around the room. Jojo exits out the barracks.

"You men make sure you look your best tonight and don't forget to wash behind your ears." Comforted Julio.

The Filipino gentlemen who are ready for the night begin to help out the other Filipino men slowly getting themselves dressed up and looking clean and sharp.

Julio begins to write song lyrics and then sing to his roommates while everyone gets freshened up for the nights festivities and the Manila dance hall, I call this song, "*Hard Life.*"

Labour, let's talk about the labour
Labour, let's talk about the labour
Na na na na Hard life
Labour labour
Force, force - I feel just like a force
Na Hard life
Like a force
But I got more stronger
Stronger stronger
Like a force

Hard life

Stronger stronger

Ooh, when I go ploughing

Will you hold me tight and not go labouring

I'm plowing 'til the morn

I miss your hearts

Don't be afraid to try grinding

Na na na na Hard life

Don't be afraid to try harvesting

Hard life

Hard life

But I've tried fishing before

Hard life

You must think I'm higher

I'm way too good at maneuvering

Don't be afraid to try strengthening

Hard life

Strengthening strengthening

And I'm dancing because you're rife dancing because it's relaxing

It's time we had some classes

Na na na na Hard life

Will you hold me tight and not go entrenching

Rising and rife

Life life

Don't be afraid to try bulldozing

I feel skillful

I need a peerless break

A daybreak for you and me

A peerless break

All the Filipinos around the area in the room are all whistling a melody to the song as a few of the other Filipinos follow in and whistle along in unison. "Sing us another Julio, you got another good song in you while we all get ready for tonight's dancing? Get us in the mood!" says Conrado as he is laying out his clothes onto his bed while only wearing his underwear, undershirt, socks and its suspenders on each leg.

Julio says, "let me see my journal I think I wrote a couple of new ones that sounds good, found it! Ok let me test this one out for your ear holes boys, the name of this song is *A Watsonville California State of Mind*."

Yeah, yeah

Ayo, Americans, it's time.

It's time, Americans (aight, Americans, begin).

Straight out the fun islands of the Philippines.

My music drops deep as does my goat kambing.

I love to dance, 'cause to dance is the kaunaan of all.

Beyond the oceans of Filipinos, life is defined.

I think of dancing when I'm in a Watsonville California state of mind.

Hope this song got some fit.

My wit don't like no dirty banana split.

Run up to the hall get your dance on.

In a Watsonville California state of mind.

What more could you ask for? The good dance? Good harvest.

You complain about rioting.

I gotta love it though - somebody still speaks from the hip on the Flip.

I'm farming in the day,

And dancing that body at night.

Abundant, rich, well dressed, clean from farming

Boy, I tell you, I thought you were a rooster wake me up in the morning.

I can't take the Rioting, can't take the smashing.

I woulda tried to sing and play music I guess I got no real freedom got to work

for it.

I'm farming in the day,

And dancing that body at night.

Yea, yaz, in a Watsonville California state of mind.

When I was young my manong had a farm.

I got but kicked because of jealousy.

I never thought I'd see that firearm.

Ain't a soul alive that could take my manong's disarm.

A fantastic gamble is quite the preamble.

Thinking of Dancing. Yaz, thinking of Dancing (Dancing) is on my mind.

The Filipino bunkmates erupt in cheers and applause, "Very good! Very good! Thank you Lord well said Julio," said Conrado ecstatically gives Julio a high five, "Amazing boy very creative."

Jojo brings in the mail into the room and distributes it, "We got mail!" He hands a couple of envelopes out and then arrives at Gerald's envelope. "Ahhh Gerald. Here Gerald mail for you." Jojo hands Gerald his mail as he passes out the rest of the handful of mail that was delivered to their farm campgrounds.

Gerald begins to read the letter he got as the rest of the other boys get ready for the nights festivities. Gerald from a distance begins to slowly cry as tears fall down from his eyes down his face.

It's very rare when this happens when you get a letter from home saying that one of your loved ones has passed away into heaven, in this case Gerald's father in the Philippines. Only five days they found him in the fields with rice still in his mouth it looks like he may have been dead for five days before anyone had found him.

All the boys in the room console their friend Gerald as he cries away. "Why lord?"

Surrounded by his Filipino housemates. One at a time they pat Gerald's head showing their respect and condolences and then one by one they each begin to

148

get dressed up for the night's festivities leaving Gerald to himself for some time alone.

The last to leave Gerald's side is Julio. "I am sorry to hear of the news of your father Gerald. He is in a better place now and so are you, I'm sure he is looking over you and hopefully all of us. You are in a better place as well you get to dance with all these fine American women. Come on get ready for tonight. I will buy you a dance."

A smile comes across Gerald's face, 'Thank you Manong. You are the best!"

They shake hands and Gerald blesses Julio's hand on to his forehead. Christian crosses Gerald and Julio's paths and is met halfway in between with Jojo and they do a cool dance moves.

"You have got to do this dance move tonight kuya," said Christian as he shows his best dance move.

"When you do that dance move kuya you will probably get a free dance." Laughed Jojo.

Laughter and smiles shared among all the Pinoy's in the camp bunkhouse.

"Sing us a new song or you have a nice poem pare you can share with us Julio? For old times sake tama right?" said Jojo, standing up on the table.

"Why thank you Jojo I would love too ok the name of this song is that is *Why Mr. Gerald is a Great Farmer!*" shouted Julio, trotting along the wooden floor of the bunkhouse singing.

Have you met Mr. Gerald Emano?
Someone said as we shook hands.
He was just Mr. Gerald to me.

Then I said, "Mr Gerald,
You're a gentleman who understands,
I'm a man who must be a singing dancer."

"'You better eat vegetables, you better not throw stones,
You better not drink liquor, I'm telling you why,
New Filipino farm worker recruit is coming to Watsonville!
New Filipino farm worker recruit is coming to Watsonville!
New Filipino farm worker recruit is coming, coming to Watsonville."

I practiced farming, dancing, writing and singing every day,
To find some clever lines to say,
To make the meaning come through...

And then I went and spoiled it all, by saying something stupid like:
"I will own a ranch someday be a ranchero."

I can see it in his eyes, that he despises death,
Like the day before.

He loves father,
He hates the hard life,
He loves dancing.

That's why Mr Gerald,

That's why Mr Gerald Emano,

That's why Mr. Gerald is a Great Farmer!

I will own a ranch one day be a ranchero.

I will be a great farmer someday!

The Filipino bunkmates are screaming loud, "Hip hip hooray Pare! That sounded great!" Gerald immediately rushes towards Julio sticking his hand out and shaking his hands giving a big hug, "Thank you Julio that was beautiful, simply beautiful I needed to hear that," said Gerald raising both fists into the air in celebration and victory.

At night Gerald, Julio, Jojo, Christian, Boy, Soriano, Conrado, Binong, and remaining group of Pinoy's wait outside the doors of the Manila dance hall waiting for it to open.

"Hey gentlemen it is time to go in." Exclaimed Gerald.

Many Filipinos are already waiting in line to get into the dance hall. As from a distance towards the end of the line a large group of white townsman approach the Manila dance hall.

Inside the Manila dance hall the festivities are going on in full energy as the big band orchestra plays to the music beats of all the dancing partners on the dance floor. Guys are flashing their dollar bills as a nearby woman grabs it and stashes it into her bra.

At the gambling tables Christian with his female date for the evening are playing poker with four other Pinoy's and their dates massaging their shoulders while the dealer's cards are dealt out as everyone places their minimum initial bets in the middle of the pot of the table.

On the dance floor Julio with a pocket full of tickets is dancing with Joy.

Julio hands a dance ticket to Joy. Big Country and a couple of white townsman dressed up and

cleaned up nice survey the dance floor not seeing Joy and Julio because a crowd of dancers is blocking them. Julio dancing with Joy enjoying themselves. Julio twirls around Joy.

Julio and Joy now at a steady dance pace while catching their breath.

"You're a great dancer. It's Julio right? That's your name Julio?" Admired Joy. The red light flashes turns on in the room. Julio gives Joy another dance ticket that she places in her bra. Big Country Townsman and two of his white townsman boys comes close to Julio but with each others backs towards each other they don't see each other as Julio sees them from the corner of his eyes he adjusts himself with his back completely towards them. Big Country townsman and

his two white townsman boys walk off the dance floor and towards the gambling table area.

The red light flashes and lights up the room again. Julio hands another dance ticket to Joy and Joy places the ticket in her bra.

"That was a close call." Sighed Julio.

'What do you mean?" Consoled Joy.

'Oh nothing let us keep dancing." Reassured Julio.

"Boy those dance moves Julio got you some type of energy man." Shouted Joy. Her and Julio are dancing in each other's arms. Twirling and dipping each other. Looking into each other's eyes. Puppy eyes. He strokes and plays with her hair.

The dance floor becomes more crowded. Looking like only elbow room only on the dance floor.

Julio is talking to Joy whispering into her ear while he sees Big Country Townsman a few yards away in the gambling tables.

At the gambling table area enters the tall and monstrous Big Country Townsman "Where is that one Filipino monkey at?'

"Sir honestly it is going to be hard to find him in here because everyone looks the same like all these other monkeys." Declared White Townsman Joe Two.

On the packed dance floor Julio talking into Joy's ear. "Why, thank you madam. I appreciate it and your kind words. Beautiful.'

Joy pulling outwards arms distance away looking straight into Julio's eyes.

"Beautiful? Who are you calling beautiful Sir? You must tell everyone that to every girl you lay our eyes on." Admired Joy.

Julio talks into Joy's ear cupping his hands. "No ma'am I think you're the most beautiful woman I have ever seen on earth. Of course next to my mother and your mom."

The red light flashes and lights up the room. Julio checks his pockets. With his hands open to his side. He has no more dance tickets as Joy watches on.

"I'll have to get more tickets Joy. Until next time. Goodbye." Insisted Julio. As soon as there hands part ways. A new Filipino dance patron hands a dance ticket to Joy. Looking towards Julio she places the dance ticket in her bra.

153

Julio walks backwards towards the bar while looking at Joy distances way. He blows a kiss towards Joy into the sky. Julio turns around and walks up to the bar.

Joy grabs the kiss from the air but Julio does not see it as he keeps walking away.

At the bar area Julio walking up to the bar he is met up with Jojo. While at the bar with Julio is his friend Jojo who is enjoying a drink together.

"Lets toast pare! I will get you another drink." Shouted Jojo.

"No thank you Kuya save your money. " Yelled Julio.

"That's ok we get paid next week hopefully again. What's a matter?" Reassured Jojo.

"Why are you here in America Kuya?" Comforted Julio.

'The Freedom... I want to go to school here but our pay is not enough to live on and save to go to college. So I just live day by day." Continued Jojo.

People are partying it up and dancing from a distance the other side of the hall room gambling is taking place at the tables while Julio and Jojo are talking it up at the crowded bar. With a couple of the white townsman crew working behind the bar counter one of them takes an eye into Julio and gives a shoulder what's up head gesture to a fellow white townsman crew member working alongside that Julio is in the building.

"So why you here in America for Julio?" Shouted Jojo.

With a drink already in his hand Julio takes a sip of his drink taking a few moments before he answers that question. Jojo orders a couple coca cola soda pops for Julio and himself.

"I believe I am here in America to make a fortune, to make a difference, to change the world by simply surviving, maybe start a family and definitely become the best professional dancer in town as a start." Declared Julio.

Jojo laughing as he slightly spills his soda pop while other Filipinos are conversing with

each other and playing drinking games.

"What's that saying it's free to dream. Pare you don't want to become a martyr do you? A saint? Don't kill yourself while doing it." Laughed Jojo.

The two finally get their Coca cola, Jojo takes out his metal flask and pours a little bit into their colas and they do a cheers.

"I'm just being me pare. To a great life!" Shouted Julio.

6

Gambling, Riots, Liquor, Discrimination.

The next day on the farm fields Julio, Jojo, Christian, Conrado, Gerald, Binong, Boy, Soriano and his Filipino campmates continue to work hard on the fields. Working together on a field with at least a hundred yards to work on left to go for the day.

Julio leads the pack of Filipino men following his ways of attending to the farmland.

Since Julio got that letter from his ex-girlfriend who went off and married another Filipino back home it looks like he was determined to face his challenges.

Working the fields Julio takes a breather, "that's it guys I'm going to get married to a white woman and go to North Carolina or Louisiana. I here it is fine to get married in those states."

All the Filipino men within Julio's vicinity completely stand up right from what Julio just said.

"You know that's illegal here in America now don't you? You'd go to jail. You know!" Declared Christian.

Jojo picking at the ground comes up right directing his attention to Julio.

"You can always put on some lemon peels on your skin to cleanse whitten it to keep your dark skin light as white!" Laughed Jojo.

"I got a poem for that right there pare take a listen real quick the name of the poem is *Jojo's Torment of the Lemon*," says Julio trotting along the dirt grove.

Jojo couldn't stop thinking about the lemon
It was just so whitener and yellow
But he could never forget the freshness clean smell

That morning, Jojo was shocked by the hemmen
He had to calm himself with some cologne
Jojo couldn't stop thinking about the lemon

Later, Jojo was spooked by a white man

156

He tried to focus on a dancing woman
But he could never forget the deep flehmen

Conrado tried to distract him with a lemon
Said it was time to start thinking about another hobby
Jojo couldn't stop thinking about the lemon

Jojo took action like a dancer
The lemon was like a toxic evil mobster
But he could never forget the riots

Jojo nosedived like a yellow lemon to the ground
His mind turned into a montebello
Jojo couldn't stop thinking about the clean lemon
But he could never forget the fighting during the riots

"What kind of poem was that pare interesting nice rhythm ok alright we best get back to work now" shouted Jojo. Everyone laughs in unison and gets back to working the fields. The Filipino farm workers working the fields like a well-oiled machine assembly line.

As the workday comes to a close and the sun still shining bright the many Filipino gentlemen farm workers walk by a wooden shack with a long line of farmers forming waiting for their turn to go inside the shack.

Life in America at this time was lonely so sometimes after a long day of hard work the Filipino farm workers couldn't help but wait in long lines in front of a shack for a quick massage by the female farm attendants.

A teenage boy a few yards away towards the end of the line sits on the dirt road on top of a rock reading his book as Julio, Jojo, Christian, Conrado, Gerald, Binong, Boy, Soriano and the rest of his bunk housemates pass by. Julio shares his new poem with the gentlemen, "Gentlemen I have a new poem I would like to share with you, is it ok to share with all of you?" his bunk housemates look at each other to see if this is a good time, "Yeah sure go ahead Julio." Said Conrado, "Say it with feeling and emotion." The guys just all laugh as Julio says, "Great alright then the name of my new poem is *Life In* Beautiful America."

Life in Beautiful America
Farming by early day rise
Dancing by night time
With Dime A Dance American Dames
Their Passion for Dime a Dance is Oh So Nice

Life in Beautiful America
Farming by day rise
Rest day is really on Sunday
But how will I have more money I will work harder to
Dime A Dance If I can Once Again

Life in Beautiful America

Farm by day
A Farm for Four Seasons
Dancing is what I live for taking it day by day
Saving is hard for what do we save for

Life in Beautiful America
Acres of Farms
Wish I be a dancing ranchero someday
Till then I will dance the night away. Getting Better Every Single Day.

Moaning and movement noises can be heard coming out from the shack that the bunk house mates are passing.

"Ahhhh I'm sooo happy." Yelled a male voice from the shack. The Filipino farm workers outside look at each other and cant help but laugh.

A Filipino farm worker comes out of the shack with a big smile on his face and the white female attendant sticking her leg outside the door and brings it in with now only her arm index finger gesturing to come on in.

From inside the shack "Ok boys who is next? Come to paradise," whispered the White Female Attendant.

The next Filipino farm worker attendant takes a step and turns to his fellows in line and salutes them as he skips into the shack.

On the dirt ground from behind the farm's barn Julio sees as he is walking towards the back side of the barn a couple of Filipino guys and an audience of people around them with two rooster cock fighters about to attack each other.

With a few rooster gamecocks still in their cages Julio approaches a near by white owner near a cage of his rooster cock fighters.

"These your roosters?" Exclaimed Julio. The owner nods yes.

"How much for your best cock fighter sir?" Shouted Julio.

The owner tosses his hands up to his side like he doesn't know. Julio gives his money from his pockets and pays the owner and takes the rooster fighter out of the cage and gets it

ready for the next fight on deck.

A couple of his bunkhouse mates make pre bet wagers.

Julio takes his rooster into the main arena he lifts it into the air and displays it for the crowd.

The Fight begins. The two roosters fly at each other in fighting action. Julio's rooster wins.

Julio gets paid his money from the bookie cashier manager with cash in hand. "Awesome! Now I have enough money to dance with Joy the night away!" The referee raises Julio's arm and his rooster in the air in victory.

In the evening at the Manila dance hall Julio, Jojo, Christian, Conrado, Gerald, Binong, Boy, Soriano and other nearby Filipino camp farm workers all cleaned up in their suits make their way to the cashier dance ticket booth with cash in their hands ready to buy up dance tickets. A long line has already formed as Jojo, Julio and rest of his bunkhouse mates line up for dime a dance tickets.

Julio counts his money and places it back into his pockets.

"Now Julio please don't go on a wasting all your money on dance tickets pare. It's not worth it save it for a good meal or a cola for you ok? Promise me that!" Yelled Jojo.

"Just counting my earnings today. You're right Jojo! I'll only use half and save the rest." Shouted Julio.   He decides to save some of his money and places it in his coat inner pocket. As the line gets moving Filipinos who have their dance tickets already walk steadily past Julio with excitement in their faces.

The Dance hall dance floor doors are now open. Julio finally gets to the front of the line.

Julio grabs his tickets from the cashier and rushes to the dance floor and he notices Joy has just entered the dance hall. Julio rushes to her side and offers his dance ticket to her and they dance the night away ticket after dance ticket given to Joy. The night is over as Julio gives her his last dance ticket to Joy. They say goodbye.

Later that night Julio, Jojo, Christian, Conrado, Gerald, Binong, Boy, and Soriano are walking back to their bunkhouse after a night of dancing. Slowly dragging their feet They walk up an approaching dimly lit intersecting fork in the road just as two cars lights approach the intersection at a normal rate a car is blocking their passage through with Big Country Townsman and a couple of his white townsmen, they jump out and get out of the car blocking their way and form a straight diagonal line shoulder with apart while they bat their sticks on the palm of their hands.

"You monkeys go back where you came from. Go on now walk back. No dogs allowed going through this way here." Yelled Big Country Townsman.

Julio and his bunk house mates walk backwards picking it up making a sudden dash and split up sprint into the different directions quickly getting out of the vicinity of the white townsman's view. The sounds of them running through the fields.

"Sir them Filipino monkey's sure are quick and fast." White Townsman Joe Two.

Nothing but dirt dust is up in the air from the running away of the Filipino farm workers.

"You can say that again they can really pick up the dust." Laughed Big Country Townsman.

The white townsman crew coughs up from the dust left from the sudden quick speed escape of the Filipino bunkmates.

The next day on the farm fields with the sun rising over the east as Julio, Jojo, Christian,

Conrado, Gerald, Binong, Boy, and Soriano and the rest of his bunkhouse mates are passed out on the ground lying on top of each other like pillows. All snoring and breathing deep and loud. Sound asleep. Like an orchestra snoring and breathing. Breathing and snoring deeply loud.

Flies buzzing around the sleeping Filipino farm workers. Julio waking up to the combination of the sun beaming against his eyes lids and the noise of the roosters by the barnyard on the side dirt road adjacent to the farm fields that they work on.

"What a night gentlemen. Huh? Wake up guys! Time to work!" Declared Julio. The rest of the guys get up gingerly stretching out their bodies for the morning stretch.

"Is today payday?" Shouted Jojo.

"Why you going to keep womanizing those white woman again with all you allowance money Jojo?" Consoled Julio.

Dusting himself off and dusting off the dirt off of Julio.

162

"I got nothing to live for pare." Mumbled Jojo.

Julio dusts off any dirt on Jojo. The same goes for the rest of the Filipino farm workers copying what Julio and Jojo do.

That night at the Manila dance hall white women were seen sitting on the laps of Filipino men.

As a few of the white townsmen crew works from behind the bar start keeping an eye on the party people. Jojo is talking to a woman, he tips her, and she proceeds to give him a shoulder and neck massage. Jojo looking towards Julio who is waiting for his turn to dance. Julio gestures to Jojo calls him out.

"Save your money pare." Consoled Julio.

Jojo points too the direction to go on the dance floor and gives a thumbs up to Julio. He waves at Jojo as he keeps waiting to dance with an available woman to dance with. The dance ticket cashier patron approaches Julio.

"Need a dance ticket Sir?" Exclaimed Ticket Cashier.

Julio gives the patron all of his money in his pocket one dollar at a time but takes his last

one dollar and places back in his pocket.

"Thank you!" Shouted Julio.

Julio keeps an eye on any woman available yet to dance as Joy is still dancing with another Filipino man on the dance floor.

"Boy that is a lot tickets you sure?" Said the Ticket Cashier.

Julio places the remaining dance tickets into his coat pockets.

At the poker gambling tables Conrado, Christian, Boy, Soriano, a Japanese guest and a Chinese house dealer is gambling and playing card games of poker. The pot of cash is pretty large with a pile in one particular group table.

Conrado looks at his cards on hand, places them down, to check his pockets if he has more cash to increase his bet. Conrado finds his last dollar.

"Here goes my luck, there it goes." Maintained Conrado. He throws it into the pile of dollars.

"Minimum bets in gentlemen. Some words from the wise. Don't spend all your seasons earnings tonight!" White House Dealer.

Conrado, Christian, Boy, and Soriano look at each other in amazement on what the house dealer has said.

"Right on. I am the master of my fate the captain of my soul." Commanded Conrado.

"Wow what is that Shakespeare?" Declared House dealer. The house dealer shuffles the cards, halves the deck and shuffles the cards again. He places the deck in front of Conrado.

"Cut please." Comforted House Dealer. Conrad halves the deck and stacks it up "Thank you." House dealer then deals out the cards.

On the dance floor that evening with an entire roll of tickets in his hands Julio waits for his turn in line as their is a long line of other Filipinos waiting to dance with only a few white woman.

Julio notices Joy from a distance still dancing with a fellow Pinoy brother. A crowd of Filipino on lookers people watching, drinking Coca - Cola and making cheering noises rooting for their favorites as the big band orchestra plays on. The red light flashes. Pinoy's with no more dance tickets leave their white female dance partner counterparts and a new batch of Filipinos replace their hands in a dance or two or more.

The fellow Pinoy brother that was dancing with Joy runs out of dance tickets and leaves a kiss on Joy's hand and gestures a goodbye. The Pinoy brother standing behind Julio taps Julio on the shoulder because Julio was counting his tickets one by one he points Julio to Joy's direction, as he is to be the next dance partner.

"Looks like you'll be dancing the entire night pare? She looks ready for you." Laughed Pinoy brother.

"We will see. Tonight is the night, could be no tomorrow!" Gushed Julio. He is escorted to Joy who smiles at Julio.

Back at the gambling tables music can be heard in full swing. The clock on the wall says two O'clock ante meridian morning time as workers clean up after the place.

Smiles on the Filipino gentlemen's faces as they finish up their last minute dances with the Caucasian women dime dancing hostesses.

"Last call for drinks, last bets, last dance ladies and gentlemen. Thank you for coming. And to all a pleasant safe night." Sighed the Master of Ceremonies. The place is still bustling as the dancing people finish their last drinks before the last musical dance number.

A storm of white townsman rage into the dance hall and begin rioting the entire place.

Music stops.

Screaming.

Dance floor people scatter around for safety. Conrad finds safety behind the bar counter, takes the Coca-Cola from the bar and drinks it fast, places it back on top of counter and dashes out of the area.

Punches are thrown and exchanged.

Jojo, Christian, Gerald, Binong, Boy, and Soriano together quickly escape out the front entrance. Tables are tossed and turned over. People are being pushed and thrown. Julio grabs the hand of Joy as they sprint out of the dance hall amid the flying chairs and glasses.

"Come on let us get out of here Joy. Come with me!" Yelled Julio.

Very late at night early morning on the farm fields Julio and Joy find refuge and escape out on a full moon. It shines upon the ground that they lay. Julio lays down his jacket so they both take a rest from running away quickly.

Joy resting her head on this chest. In each other's arms cuddling. Her head on his chest. Suddenly the dame stands up as he follows so also.

"I must get back before they come find the both of us together here." Exclaimed Joy. She leaves quickly but not as quick as Julio grabs hold of her hand and pulls her body close to his face looking into her eyes.

"You have the most beautiful pretty eyes. Sure sweetheart, darling you're right, rest real quick and catch your breath." Whispered Julio.

Looking into each other's eyes.

Julio plays with her hair. Slightly touches the side of her face. "I wrote a new song for you well it is about you, can I sing it to you?" insisted Julio.

"I am speechless really Julio." says Joy acting all surprised covering her mouth in the mystery and looking at Julio's live one on one performance he is saying, "Ghh..Ghh..Me..Me..Me.. Ok ready! A One, A Two, A One, Two.."

I farm all day, dance all night long got more tickets,
I smile dancing the right way, here I am to say that I love you.

You're wholly beautiful, wholly Molly, wholly marvelous to me.

Best part of dancing, you stepped onto the floor, moved my feet let me see
Belle that made this body adore you, dream of a living consumed with you
Prince of all days, oh so hot dancer, celebrated on dance floor
Modestly you smelling like the world you created, all for love's sake became
rich
Also I'll nay see whereby enough chemistry value into view mi vice
simultaneous one irritable

I farm all day dance all night long got more tickets,
You have the prettiest eyes I have ever seen,
I smile dancing the right way, here I am to say that I love you.
You're wholly beautiful, wholly molly, wholly marvelous to me.

Joy clapping her hands in Joy and yelling, "Bravo! Bravo! Bravo! Encore
please! Again! Again!"
"Really? Ok I will sing you new song I wrote about you listen, the song is
called, *"Our Great Dancer Asparagus Love."*
This one's for you Miss Bailey!

My love for you is like the most great dancer who eats asparagus,
Your face reminds me of friendly fish swing in the rivers of Sacramento,
Together, we are like whole chicken and ketchup.

Oh darling Joy,
My great dancer asparagus,
My friendly lettuce,
The perfect companion to my whole chicken soul.

Tomatoes are red,
Eyes are blue,
I like dance halls,
But not as much as I love dancing with you!

Oh darling Joy,
Your hands are like beautiful papers on a spring day oh my oh my I like to write,
You're like the most kind doctor to ever walk into a Manila dance hall in history.

Your friendly fish face,
Your ketchup soul,
Your beautiful hands,
Your kind doctor being...

How could I look at another when our great dancer asparagus love is so strong?

I love you Miss Bailey! Magandang gabi!

Thank you and all a good night!

"What is that *Magandang Gabi*? whispered Joy as she has not heard of that word before wanting to learn more about Julio and where he came from.

"Oh that madam Joy means in the Filipino Tagalog language is good night or good evening." Julio explaining the translation to Joy.

"Ok that is what it means, I love it, it is beautiful, that is great Julio. Thank you for sharing such nice words with me." Joy looks around to see if no one is within their site for they can not be caught seen together in public.

Julio then all of a sudden gets down on his knees.

"Will you marry me Joy? Shouted Julio.

"Shhh! Be quiet! They will hear us! Are you kidding? They will kill you! You are a great dancer and a true all handsome gentlemen." Whispered Joy as she is covering Julio's mouth with her palm of her hands.

Julio gets up. They kiss.

"I got to go! Kindly please give me space." Whispered Joy.

She quickly runs off just as Julio grabs her hand

"Goodbye Joy!" Sighed Julio.

Joy and Julio kiss one last time. They let go. Catching their breath. Breathing out loud.

Holding each other's hands at arms distance. Embracing the moment. Holding each other tight hugging whispering into each other's ear.

"We better get back before anyone notices us. You know it is against the law for us to be together right?" Urged Joy.

The sound of a nearby cow makes moans and moos sounds. So quiet now you can hear the crickets chirping in the background. A clear night full of bright shiny stars. A star falls from the sky.

"Alright! I'd be complete if we can have just one last dance together." Sighed Julio

In each other's arms Joy lays her head on Julio's shoulder as they slow dance. A couple of twirls and one last dip. Julio brings Joy up. Breathing deeply. A noise of rustled leaves moving comes from a few yards away from where they stand. One last look into each other's eyes. They run off into different directions.

Julio runs towards a barn shack ahead of him and arrives out of breath walking and he notices a leather basketball next to the barn. He picks it up, tosses it in the air a couple times.

Makes circles with the ball around his waist. Twirls into the air, and spins it on his index finger, looks at it and bounces it once and then a second time. He notices no one is around, takes a walk circles around the barn, looking for a comfortable safe place, he takes refuge and rests laying his head on the ball on the other side of the barn with another farm camp at a distance. Looking up into the clear stars shining bright night. The big dipper. The north star in clear sites view.

"I used to shine shoes in the Philippines and work on the farm and this right here has prepared me for my American dream that I'm living now God really?" Insisted Julio.

A star falls from the sky.

"Give me wisdom lord!" Declared Julio. I thank you for my freedom but why does my freedom feel like I'm a criminal and that crime is that I'm Filipino? Let me write a song I think there is enough light out here tonight that I can see my pen and paper, let's do it." He takes out his pen and paper out of his suit coat jacket gets it directly underneath the moons lighted area from the sky he begins to write whispering to himself, "I will name this song and title it *Fun to Dance.*"

Dancing shoes with banjo guitars

I dance in your arms

Truly dancing fantastic

Like fantastic banjo guitars

We shall dance

Fun to dance

Smells like a fantastic banjo guitars

Let's run away to America and dance with banjo guitars

The beauty of your farm lands

Banjo guitars in my farm

They are night banjo guitars! They have come back from America!! Ahhhh!

Harvest my farm up

Joy's waiting

Born fantastic

Like a farm

Banjo guitars sound better with you

Fun to dance

Great banjo guitars of farm

I want to play my fantastic banjo guitars

Farm deep groves, banjo guitars strung right

Your fantastic heart

Whole lotta fantastic banjo guitars

Bridge over fantastic banjo guitars

A lot of people tell me I have a fake farm

Rhythm of the farm

Dance forever

America is your land

The girl from America

I dance

Fun to dance

This is a sight we had one day from fantastic America

Living on a farm

Baby, I need your banjo guitars

Straight outta of the Philippines to America

Stairway to farm lands

It's the beginning of America as we know it feeling fine and glorious

My farm sounds better with you in it

Can't take my banjo guitars off of you

You think I ain't worth a farm but I feel like a million banjo guitars

Smells like a fantastic farm

Yearning for fantastic banjo guitars

Early morning farm

Bed of banjo guitars

Ring of farm groves

America on my mind

Stand by our banjo guitars

Mammas don't let your babies grow up to be banjo guitars

Your working on the farm

There's a good reason banjo guitars are numbered, Joy

Farm I have become one

Amazing Joy

Don't dance, dance more

Fun to dance

Stairway to America

Welcome to fantastic America

Farm lands and more farm lands

Look Joy, are you going to dance with me or not?

At least give me my banjo guitars back, you go dance on the farm!

Work in my farm

Takin' the farm train

Joy eat my fantastic potatoes from the farms in America

Farm fields forever

Dance? I jolly well will dance for your eyes only

Fun to dance

Late night on the farm

My fame is Joy

Somewhere over the farm

Another year of banjo guitars

Sweet farm of mine

In farm we trust

Stand by Joy

You've got that fantastic feeling

Careful with that farm

She thinks Filipino farm workers are sexy

Independent farmers

Good old America

You don't send me fantastic banjo guitars anymore

Good farm lands

A song for Joy

Whole lotta banjo guitars

My farm wants to kill our man working hard all day for little pay

Where have all the banjo guitars gone?

Stand by your farm

Hey Joy

Just another a fantastic farm

Free farm

I plead farm

Here without Joy

Joy broke my heart at America

Many pieces of large fuzzy banjo guitars gathered together at America and

grooving

on

A farm

Goody two banjo guitars

Nice weather for banjo guitars

House of the fantastic farm

Look Joy, this is my farm

When fantastic banjo guitars dance

Behind fantastic banjo guitars

Dance, dance, dance!

Fun to dance

You can't dance through a buffalo herd

Have you met Joy?

Fantastic dancer

When fantastic banjo guitars play all night

Play more of that banjo guitars a little bit more

One angry farm manager and two hundred fantastic Filipino banjo guitar players

Dance - It is the most fun a girl can have

Julio shakes his head and stretches his arms, hands and wrists from all the work he did in writing another song, feeling good, relieved it is time to get some shut eye and rest for the night.

He starts falling asleep. He closes his eyes and starts to have a dream.

Dreaming of himself as a young looking Julio in the farm fields of the Philippines. Riding a Carabao (Water Buffalo) on a vast farm field and all of a sudden he falls off it.

Back in the barn shack Julio wakes up opening his eyes from his real quick dream by the neighboring white farm property owner who throws a bucket of water on Julio getting drenched soaking wet.

"Hey good morning son don't worry I'm a good guy. Are you ok? How you living?" Comforted neighboring white farm property owner. He throws some new clothes over to Julio's side and a towel. Julio sits right up and gets up on his feet quickly, "thank you." Squeezing off any excess water from his clothes.

"You know you shouldn't be sleeping around late at night on other people's property son. Go ahead and rinse yourself off and dry yourself around the corner. " Says the Neighboring White Farm Property Owner. Around the barn Julio takes a shower in the wooden makeshift outhouse bath comfort room. Towels off, changes into his new fresh farm workers outfit. Neighboring White Farm Property Owner approaches Julio with his old clothes.

"I am just trying to survive sir sought quick shelter for the night that's all thank you. I'll get going to work now. Excuse me. Good day. Thank you again. I appreciate it!" Admired Julio.

Julio hands towel to Neighboring White Farm Property Owner. They shake hands and salute each other along their way.

Later that morning on the farm fields Julio arrives alone as the rest of his housemates are already attending to the farm work.

"You're late pare. Where have you been?" Blurted Jojo.

From a distance behind while the Filipino farm workers attend to the fields, Big Country Townsman approaches the field manager. The Filipino farm workers keep working on the farm field while the two are conversing. The field manager gestures and waves ok for Big Country townsman to approach the group of Filipino farm workers.

"I was lost last night, so I took cover at a nearby barn." said Julio.

The Big Country Townsman approaches Julio and the rest of the Filipino farm workers.

"Julio?" Declared Big Country Townsman.

Julio and his Filipino work mates raise their backs up one at a time. Julio steps to the side to be in full view a few yards away.

"I am Julio Sir." Declared Julio.

"I challenge you to a dancing duel!" Laughed Big Country Townsman. He sticks out his huge solid rock hard arms hand pulsating with veins bulging his index finger pointing at Julio. Julio walks towards Big Country Townsman, looks up to him, salutes him and shakes his hand.

Julio standing in front of a hundred other Filipino farm workers facing the lone Big Country Townsman. Julio and Big Country Townsman make eye contact. Steaming, huffing and puffing. Slow deep breaths. Julio takes a bow down to Big Country Townsman and rises up.

"Sir, you are challenging me to a dancing duel?" Laughed Julio. Big Country Townsman nodding his head up and down.

"How will we live that moment out? What will be the rules?" Declared Julio.

Big Country begins to walk along and facing looking at each other the farm workers starting with Julio then in front of Jojo, Conrado, Gerald, Binong, Christian, Boy Isagani and

Soriano behind him.

"Whoever can raise the most dance tickets to dance and can dance the longest without cramping or injury can be declared the best dance champion!" Reassured Big Country Townsman

Big Country Townsman walking back ending in front of Julio face to face.

Julio looking back at his fellow farm workers and campmates. They nod yes and each one gives Julio a salute one at a time. "One condition, no more riots Sir! Yelled Julio.

"Deal let us shake on it!" Said Big Country Townsman.

Big Country Townsman and Julio both shake hands on the dancing duel deal.

That night the Filipino farm housemates calmly and peacefully sound asleep. Snoring loud one after the other breathing deeply.

At the farm camp grounds next door a couple of White Townsman covered in dark clothing quietly walks up, sets down and lights up a couple sticks of dynamite on the sides and entrance of the Filipino farm camp next door.

A thunderous loud boom sound outside explodes. Ball of Fire lights up the sky of the next-door farm camp the bunkhouse next door is on fire. Someone is running away from the fire.

Nextdoor Christian hears the loud boom and gets up out of his sleeping cot. "What was that?"

One after the other Julio, Jojo, and the rest of Filipino bunk house mates get up.

"We're under attack its the other Filipino bunk house exploded on the other side." Shouted Jojo.

Conrado, Gerald, Binong, Boy Isagani and Soriano wake up and get up. Running outside their door following one another. Sprinting as fast as they can across the field while looking at the fire. They run towards the next-door bunkhouse. People fleeing from the burning areas.

The next morning as the sun rises over the steaming campgrounds of what is left of the fire from last night. The sound of roosters making noises crowing.

Soriano along with some Filipino farm workers make less frequent water bucket splashes on the hot black ashes of the building. Steam rises from the remaining ashes. A pale of water is thrown on the burnt wood by one of the Filipino farm workers.

"That is a good gentleman. Good job thank you." Reassured Soriano. He starts walking from around the corner of the burn down barracks approaches Julio who is walking up to the structure sees Soriano out in front of him.

"Glad you are alive Soriano." Consoled Julio.

Greeting each other with an embrace.

"So what is your next move pare?" Comforted Julio.

Following a few yards behind Julio is Jojo, Conrado, Gerald, Binong, Christian and Boy Isagani.

"I don't know, looks like the seasons work is about done here maybe. I heard there is work up up north in Seattle or Alaska in the fish canneries." Gushed Soriano.

Jojo, Conrado, Gerald, Binong, Christian and Boy Isagani greets one another all of them happy to see each other.

The next morning outside the farm bunkhouse a few Filipino farm workers taking in the outdoor recreation and relaxations as more come into the vicinity now everyone is getting their rest, relaxation and recreational activities on. Crowds of picnic people are having some cock fighting training activities inside the cockpit ring as people look onwards. Another group is doing some eskrima stick fighting drills. While another group is playing card games, as well as another group of Filipinos are drinking, another group is passing and dribbling a basketball around, while Julio, Jojo and Christian are rehearsing their dancing

179

skills, practicing it over and over again. Pausing taking a quick breather while he goes and practices his footsteps.

"Julio, you ready for your dancing duel coming up with Big Country? You got to practice show that *nakuneng* stupid guy up." Laughed Jojo.

"Yeah I got to practice so I don't look all clumsy with two left feet." Babbled Julio.

Julio showing he got the dance moves down.

Jojo doesn't look to convincing of Julio's dance moves yet.

"Yes it is looking like we have to practice somewhat more. You are getting there." Reassured Jojo.

At the eskrima practicing ground area Jojo takes Julio by the shoulder and walks to the Eskrima stick fighting training drills area that is happening close by them.

"Julio if you are going to win that dancing duel you're going to have try some different moves strengthen your multiple positions you normally don't use often. " Admired Jojo.

One of the Filipino farm workers already doing some stick drills notices Jojo and Julio coming towards him and so he gladly tosses two sticks to Jojo.

"Sir." Sighed Filipino Worker with a stick.

Jojo hands one stick to Julio as he keeps one and begins to demonstrate a drill with the stick to Julio like feng shui smooth slow dancing.

"Mix it up! That's all. Footwork and hand speed. Try the basics of Filipino stick fighting for instance." Chuckled Jojo. He demonstrates to Julio how to slowly use the stick as the woman's arm and hand. He slides the stick down his shoulder like a slide. Catches the stick and he gives the stick to Julio. He imitates how Jojo was dancing along with the eskrima stick.

"This stick is like the woman's arm and this end is the palm of her hand." Maintained Jojo.

Julio dances his dance steps with the eskrima stick.

Meanwhile at the Big Red Barn of Big Country White Townsman he opens the door to his place greets his other fellow White Townsmen checking themselves out in the mirror getting ready for the nights activities. Big Country White Townsman hides his gun in his outfit holster.

"Big man you ready to put on them dancing shoes sir?" Consoled White Townsman Joe Two.

"You gentlemen help yourself to a drink while I finish getting ready ok?" Shouted Big Country Townsman.

Everyone is completely dressed up except for Big Country White Townsman who is buttoning up his last shirt button. He grabs hold of his socks, shoes and puts them on. Then a fellow associate white townsmen hands him a tie.

Big Country White Townsman places his suit jacket on. The White Townsmen Joe Two and Big Country White Townsman check themselves out in the mirror together.

"Ok boys gather around we don't want to be late." Exclaimed Big Country Townsman

Everyone in the room gathers around Big Country Townsman.

"You guys got the map and plan on what's going to go down after tonight's dancing right? Win or lose, we're going to teach Julio and his monkey Filipinos a big lesson." Declared Big Country Townsman.

Big Country Townsman and the rest of the group White Townsmen gather around raise their glasses. "Grab a glass lets make a toast! Ok. God Bless the United States of America and those who sacrifice for our freedom!" Shouted Big Country Townsman.

Meanwhile at the dressing and makeup room of the dance hall Joy is having difficulty zipping up her back dress zipper, "Can you help me with my zipper please Missy?"

A girlfriend next to Joy zips up Joy's zipper, "Thank you sister."

Joy is looking in the mirror checking her cleavage in her dress if it is evenly covered.

Missy puts her hands on Joy's shoulders looking at her in the mirror.

"You ready for tonight? Julio going to twirl you and dip you around girl? You are going to knock him out with that dress." Laughed Missy.

Joy and her girl dime a dance doll friends are freshening up with some touch ups for the evenings dancing festivities.

"I'm ready girl bring it on." Yelled Joy.

"You are looking beautiful girl." Laughed Missy.

"Thank you Missy." Soothed Joy.

"Joy I have a question. What are Julio and his friends? They are cute and they have a lot of money girl!" Consoled Missy.

"He is Filipino from the Philippines now Americans. Yes they are. I bet they would all make good husbands but I got my eyes on that one Julio, okay girls? Make him sing you and me someday!" Babbled Joy.

A girlfriend next to Joy finds a perfume bottle shows it to Joy and she sprays some perfume on Joy.

7

Brotherhood, Dancing and Relationships

At the Filipino farm camp the bunkhouse mates and Julio are getting themselves ready for a good time after their long week of hard intense farmworking. A few of them are relaxing already kicking back with their feet up, hat covering their face napping some snoring away. One group is eating some apples. Another group is drinking toasting it up and cheering enjoying their good life.

Julio smelling the room because of its need from some freshness. He finds some cologne by his night stand of items left on top. He begins spraying some cologne on himself and into the air. Takes a sniff of the room, "smells good. Were going to be smelling good tonight men." A few of the other Filipinos near Julio take advantage of the available good smelling cologne they approach Julio as he sprays it on each one of them spraying once on each back ear lobes sharing it with each one of his nearby house work mates.

"Yeah and couple of you may even get lucky and get laid tonight!" Gushed Jojo.

Shaving their facial hair, combing their hair, the barrack housemates checking each other out making sure each one is looking sharp and dressed up for the big night of dancing.

All of them wearing sharp three piece suits about half with bow ties and the rest with regular skinny ties along with their one hundred dollar shiny shoes that they all saved up for as their first major purchase when they first arrived in America working on and caring for the beautiful farm fields.

"Tonight's the night Julio! You are going to put on a show I just know it! With your best dance moves for the gorgeous women in the dance hall *pare akko gayyem* my friend we will be cheering you right along the sidelines!" Shouted Christian. Christian and Julio give each other a hi-five.

"Oh yeah I think I'm going to do it after tonight Christian" yelled Julio who is looking pretty serious in the look of his eyes. "I heard through the grapevine that in North Carolina or Louisiana you can marry a white woman. Is that true? Have you ever heard of that law? I'm going to ask Joy to run away with me and get married." Blurted Julio.

Christian is speechless big bug eyed in amazement he can not believe what he just heard him say to him he just sticks out his hand and shakes Julio's hands, "Good luck with that brother. Best of luck man." Christian gives him a big hug saying "Come on pare I know what you need again another Cola drink!" So both Christian and Julio make their way towards the table calling out anyone of their bunk mates near by to join them in a drink ahead of them going out to dance after nightfall.

Inside the bunkhouse at the table Christian and Julio help spread out some shot glasses for the gentlemen to use for a quick drink and toast. "Come along boys gather around the table there is enough glasses for the first come first serve for this evenings refreshments for your dancing shoes before the nights cap" says Julio waving down his nearby bunk mates.

The Filipino bunk house mates mostly in their early twenties and thirties fill in to gather around the table looking perfect with their slicked back hair sharp with their dress shirts tucked in looking so fresh clean nice and wearing their neck ties a few of them with vests on for their three piece suits newly pressed with Christian and Julio situated in the middle of the long stretched dinner table that is more like a hang out spot table for the farms bunkhouse men to gather around for their inner home communal activities without having to see the pretty headshot pictures of their girlfriends from their nearby bed stands and noise of the radio playing entertainment tunes and reporting on any news worthy reports to its listeners.

That evening at the Manila dance hall Julio, Jojo, Conrado, Gerald, Binong, Christian, Boy Isagani, Soriano, house mates and other Filipino farm workers that are following behind them strut their cool dance stroll moves like it is Saturday night in unison marching down towards the towns Manila dance hall building for a night of good music and dancing. As they take their walk towards the nights festivities Julio breaks out into a song he wrote "I got a new song pare that I wrote the other night I will sing it too you as we walk ok? I dedicate this song to all the Filipino American farm workers this is for you!" The group erupts into cheers as the rest of the nearby roommates gather around to the song Julio is going to sing to them.

Here I am to you, here I am to work hard, here I am to say that you're my Manong
You're passionately strong, passionately blessed, passionately wonderful to me.
Light on the dance floor you danced stepped into love, opened my eyes let me see
Beauty that made this heart dance for you, hope of a life dancing with you.
King on the floor, oh so highly admired by the dancing queen, glorious in dance
steps
Amazed you came to this earth makes life better, all for love's sake became happy
And I'll never know how much it cost to see another dance with that girl.
Here I am to you, here I am to work hard, here I am to say that you're my Manong
You're passionately strong, passionately blessed, passionately wonderful to me and
I thank you!

"You sure you're not drunk Manong? That was great!" shouted Jojo from behind the pack of roommates following behind and pushing his way up to congratulate shake the hands of Julio for that amazing song.

186

The smell of Cola, perfume and leather can be smelt already outside of the dance hall as a long line is already forming with majority of them being Filipinos work on the farm fields as skilled laborers attending to and caring for each of the many local bonanza ranch farm land owners managers specific crops produced for the season like fruits, vegetables, cattle and dairy products from melons, lettuce, asparagus, cabbage, broccoli, collards, prickly pears, almonds, pistachios, grapes, garlic, potatoes and more tomatoes.

"Are we going to even be able to get in?" Exclaimed Conrado.

They arrive to the back of the line but unfortunately it is not moving forward. The line gets so long with now a couple hundred in line the eyes can only see and imagine.

"We better be able to get in because I got pockets of cash to give away to these ladies tonight." Stuttered Christian.

"I can not wait to start dancing already. We are going to make history tonight!" Shouted Julio.

"Yeah boys it's going to be a great night just as soon as we get in the door. We'll give them the head start so we can finish strong." Laughed Jojo.

Line still hasn't moved forward. The Filipino housemates begin to practice their dance routine footwork while they are in line to get in.

"Kind of chilly tonight no?" Gasphed Julio.

Few of the Filipinos are hopping and jumping high knees as well as cupping blowing warm air into their hands to get warmed up.

"It's going to be great Julio were going to turn up the heat inside with those fancy dancing shoes." Laughed Jojo.

Julio waiting in line to be up next to dance. He gets additional dance tickets from the

collection from the guys Conrado, Gerald, Binong, Boy, Soriano and Christian who are huddled up.

The tickets are walked over and handed to Julio by Christian. He also gets more tickets from Jojo as they all notice together that Big Country White Townsman is already dancing with Joy.

"Here's your tickets boss." Shouted Jojo. He checks his pockets finding more tickets he hands them to Julio to add to the collection. All the Filipino gentlemen looking at Big Country White Townsman doing his dance moves ahead of the pack.

"Don't worry Julio there is no competition when you know you are the best. Why don't you have a drink of cola refreshments before you make your way through the marathon dancing brother." Exclaimed Christian.

"You are right. Thank you for helping me with my confidence." Admired Julio. They do their special handshake routine of slapping hands three times then throwing their fist in the air then pointing too headed towards the bar. The line to dance is still long and has not moved yet. The red light flashes in the room signaling change of partners if they wish to do so. Big Country White Townsman eyes another female dancer and dashes to go dance with her giving her a new dance ticket.

"Here's you chance Julio. Go get em pare!" Yelled Christian.

Julio and Joy make eye contact as they both smile at each other and Julio gives her a ticket. Takes her hand kisses it and they begin to dance to the music of the orchestra. The dancing competition begins as Big Country White Townsman with his female dance partner and Julio with his dance partner Joy cross paths and start dancing next to each other for some moments seeing each other eye to eye minding each others own business.

"Ok ladies and gentlemen boys and girls tonight's the night." Babbled the Master of Ceremonies.

8

Love

Dance and jive lovers grab the hands of their dance partners as the dance floor gets more packed dancing to the musical tunes of the jive, swing and then into the rumba. A quick break is taken by most of the dancing couples heading to the bar for some cola to drink.

"We will find out who can dance till they can't dance no more." Declared the Master of Ceremonies. After their quick drinks dancing couples are back in full swing dancing the foxtrot to the tunes of the big band as the dance floor builds up to cover a sea of dancers.

The orchestra changes up their music into the samba as the red light flashes and Big Country Townsman and Julio both give dance tickets to their partner who places it in their bosoms. Julio and Joy are all smiles looking into each others eyes as Julio leads her, twirls her around and dips her towards the floor catching her safely comfortably.

Another couple shares a whisky sip break of a discretely hidden container flask wrapped inside a pocket. Others around Julio and Joy notice the amazing dance moves on display they are putting on as several couples pause dancing to admire showing some love cheering them on the best dance moves of the two.

The red light flashes Big Country White Townsman checks his pockets for more tickets.

"This can not be. I have no more tickets. Thank you ma'am for the dance." Snapped Big Country Townsman. He steps off the dance floor. As all the Filipinos dancing pass by Julio congratulating him with a roar of cheers!

Later that night Julio still dancing with Joy in her arms but down to his last ticket checking his pockets he gives cash to Christian to get more tickets for him.

"Christian here is my last money gets me as many tickets as you can with this, team work please thanks." Affirmed Julio dancing while Christian hustles back with a great amount of dance tickets.

"Here you go dance the night away Julio. You're the best!" Shouted Christian. Julio and Joy dance into the night while a crowd watches them dance together. Dance party goes on to the late hours.

At the end of the night's dancing festivities the champion dancer for the event is Julio who is getting ready gathering up his boys.

Together the Filipino band of brothers walk out full of life and energy, Julio with his Filipino bunk house mates Jojo, Conrado, Gerald, Binong, Christian, Boy, Soriano exit out the Manila dance hall.

Boom! Dynamite explodes!

190

A riot breaks out.

The sound of gunfire.

Bam! Bam! Bam!

Julio gets shot.

People gather around him as the door closes from behind them the dance hall has a new sign painted in white that reads the following:

"*NO DOGS ALLOWED AND FILIPINOS.*"

Back in present day America's Manila dance hall news media reporters surround and make room for the ninety year old grey haired Christian Portugal Abad. More media and news reporters who have arrived at Filipino time meaning they are late but just made it in time and partake in the food, refreshments and questions. Christian still in his three piece suit puts his top hat on now. He is wrapping up his story based on true events during his vivid colorful life experience of his so far so good blessed life to the public.

"We were devastated with the death of Julio and the other Filipino brothers who got killed in the riots and bombings on the farm camps during that time. So that is why you guys have it so great!" Declared Christian.

"Sorry Sir Christian what are your new stories and adventures you hope to share next?" Shouted Janelle a well known pinay reporter, host and journalist in the packed like sardines but comfortably though at the roped off stantion front stage steps of the Manila dance hall converted into a multipurpose theater stage basketball gymnasium.

"Thank you that is a wonderful question Janelle. I hope to share a series of stories in the process worlds of fiction, all genres and explore science fiction, action as well as adventure humor someday." Shared Christian with a smile on his face tipping his hat towards the crowd.

Based on true events because of that story there of Julio and the Filipino American farm workers in the period era days of the 1930's. Over 35,000 Filipinos mostly skilled farm laborers were recruited to work in the USA in hopes of fortune on the frontiers of America's farmlands inheriting a brotherhood to last a lifetime shared with you all now because they hardly had anyone to write their story until this day you have read this novel congratulations to you; they were on a mission to just work and survive here one of their proud rich heritages of the Filipino people stories.

About the Author

Abraham Gabriel Chan Pagtama

Gabe Pagtama was born in Shape, Belgium and grew up in Los Angeles, California. He attended Saint Monica's Catholic high school in Santa Monica, California and graduated with a Bachelor of Business Administration (B.B.A.) degree from Loyola Marymount University (L.M.U.) where he majored in business with an emphasis in information systems and quantitative management. His initial fascination with film and writing came at a very early age realizing that stories could be told on camera. In addition his friends and family were in the entertainment industry. Two of the major influences were his father (a lifelong actor that has been on the Conan O'Brien Show and has worked with Actor's such as Arnold Schwarzenegger, Bruce Willis, Keanu Reeves, Kim Basinger and the list goes on) and his sister who has been a career producer (her two latest projects were both Emmy Nominated "Project Runway" and "Top Chef").

Gabe Pagtama has worked in front of the camera as well as behind the camera. He has worked as an actor, writer, producer, director, and editor, which have offered multiple perspectives of the industry. His career started off at the tender age of 7 working with renowned Actor, Producer, and Director Kevin Costner in the motion picture "No Way Out". Immediately following that he was featured on a number of television series from "Highway to Heaven," "Max Headroom," "Crossing Jordan", "Monk", NBC Series "Las Vegas", CBS Series "How I Met Your Mother", and the ABC Series "Castle". He has also been on the "Conan O'Brien Show" as well as acted in numerous independent films. Amongst his many projects, he is also an Alumni of Visual Communications Armed With a Camera Fellowship for his documentary movie (Hooptown International 2006). You can view some of his short movies like *Miss Understanding* (2017) and *The Legend Of The Basketball Ghosts Short Film* (2018) Now Streaming On *Amazon.com Prime Video*

Gabe Pagtama's experience behind the camera started at the age of 8 where at which time he was using a VHS camera and was taught how to clip and edit the footage from his dad. Following that he continued to learn from his father about film all the way up until high school. In high school, with saved money from his first job, he purchased a HI-8 3 CHIP camera and enrolled in various editing classes and workshops and was able to produced his first documentary film on landlord tenant laws for business law class.

Gabe Pagtama has marketed some of the worlds top major brands and once was fortunate to be on the promotion teams for the top radio stations in Southern California like KKBT 92.3 The Beat and 102.7 KIIS FM, and is also an Entrepreneur.

Since then he has further continued his education, skills and experience having hundreds of projects under his belt. Throughout the evolution of our ever-changing technology Mr. Pagtama has upgraded his camera equipment and softwares. Throughout his career he has received numerous acknowledgements and awards. The most recent being the "Golden Halo Award" for Directing presented to him by the Film Advisor Board and the Southern California Motion Picture Council, established in 1936. The same award given in the past to the great John Wayne.

ISBN: 978-0-578-47981-1

Published by

Abraham Gabriel Pagtama and Associates

www.youtube.com/abegabe

www.marvistapictures.com

www.linktr.ee/gabepagtama

www.instagram.com/gabepagtama

www.facebook.com/agabepagtama

www.basedontrueeventsbook.wordpress.com

https://www.facebook.com/basedontrueeventsbook/

Made in the USA
Columbia, SC
12 October 2020